THE RIDERS

THE RIDERS

JACKSON COLE

THORNDIKE
CHIVERS

This Large Print edition is published by Thorndike Press, Waterville, Maine USA
and by BBC Audiobooks Ltd, Bath, England.
Thorndike Press is an imprint of Thomson Gale, a part of The Thomson Corporation.
Thorndike is a trademark and used herein under license.

The text of this Large Print edition is unabridged.
Other aspects of the book may vary from the original edition.
Set in 16 pt. Plantin.

LIBRARY OF CONGRESS CATALOGING-IN-PUBLICATION DATA

Cole, Jackson.
　　The riders / by Jackson Cole.
　　　　p. cm. — (Thorndike Press large print Western)
　　ISBN-13: 978-0-7862-9347-6 (alk. paper)
　　ISBN-10: 0-7862-9347-0 (alk. paper)
　　1. Hatfield, Jim (Fictitious character) — Fiction. 2. Texas Rangers — Fiction.
　　3. Outlaws — Fiction. 4. Texas — Fiction. 5. Large type books. I. Title.
　　PS3505.O2685R53 2007
　　813'.54—dc22　　　　　　　　　　　　　　　　　　　　　　　　　2006039155

BRITISH LIBRARY CATALOGUING-IN-PUBLICATION DATA AVAILABLE

Published in 2007 in the U.S. by arrangement with
Golden West Literary Agency.
Published in 2007 in the U.K. by arrangement with Golden West Literary Agency.

U.K. Hardcover: 978 1 405 64048 0 (Chivers Large Print)
U.K. Softcover: 978 1 405 64049 7 (Camden Large Print)

Printed in the United States of America on permanent paper
10 9 8 7 6 5 4 3 2 1

THE RIDERS

CHAPTER I
TOUGH TOWN

The crimson glow of the setting sun accentuated the red tint of the sandy earth on which stood Rusk. Named after a Texas hero, the town spread over a hilly terrain between the Neches and Angelina rivers. Southeast heavy timber growths were broken by stretches of cattle range and fields. The light glinted from the rails of two new railroads which met here, while a creek offered water.

Four saddled mustangs waited in the shade outside a roomy, long building standing off by itself from the business center and homes. A grove of second-growth longleaf pines hid the structure from the settlement's view, and through the woods ran the red-dirt lane leading to it.

The hinges holding the main door had rusted away and the portal had sagged. When it had been opened it had half fallen and its base was resting on the ground.

The men who had come on the horses were inside, standing in what had once been a busy office. Three of them faced one and there was mounting tension in the air. Fant Wright, lean in brown riding pants tucked into old boots, blue shirt and high Stetson, could sense that hostility.

Wright's gray-bearded jaw was set. It was a determined jaw, the sort a man needed to pioneer in Texas. His grim eyes riveted on Porter Daniels, obviously the leader of the trio.

"I don't cotton to yore scheme, Daniels," drawled Fant Wright. He always spoke slowly and when upset seemed to weigh every word two or three times before releasing it. "For nigh onto sixty years I've managed to stay so I can look in a mirror without bein' ashamed and I don't aim to start outlawin' now. Well, I'll mosey along." All men went armed and at Wright's hip hung an ancient horse pistol.

"Wait," ordered Daniels. "I'm the doctor. This is a cold business proposition, Wright. No sentiment in it."

Porter "Doc" Daniels was wide and heavy of body. A flattened celluloid collar graced his beefy red neck. He had plastered his thin brown hair down with grease, his forehead bulging with the unpleasant aspect of an

8

overhanging balcony. He was chewing a pencil and spoke from the other corner of his lipless mouth. He maintained the superior air of a city slicker amused by a yokel.

"Shall I grab the cuss, Doc?" asked Comanche Ben Coombs. He was a powerful figure in a range rider's rig, leather trousers and spurred boots, khaki shirt and bandanna. His hide was burned and dark to begin with. His nose bridge came out straight, then suddenly plunged down like a cliff. His high cheekbones, black eyes and dusky skin betrayed the Indian strain. Vanity showed in the upcurving sideburns and cropped dude's mustache. Two Colts, stocks patterned with gold filigree, rode in the pleated holsters while a long knife snugged against his right thigh.

"Just make sure he doesn't try any monkeyshines with that popgun, Coombsie," said Daniels.

"So that's the way it is," growled Fant Wright, stopping in his tracks en route to the exit.

The fourth man of the group was bony, his back permanently stooped. He had sharp features and his ears came to a tip. His hair was stiff as wire and he kept it cut so short the scalp showed through. He wore old garments, a pistol thrust into his belt.

"Razorback" George Kerr really had the look of the tough wild boar for which he was nick-named, and he too awaited Doc Daniels' pleasure.

"You ask too high a price for this rundown old place," declared Daniels. "I need it and don't intend to let a stupid backwoodsman stop me. I figured you might have silly ideas about throwin' in with us. That's why I was very careful how we came here. Nobody noticed us. You live alone in the piney woods and you won't be missed."

Fant Wright realized his full danger as Daniels spoke. "I'm goin' out of here, Daniels," he warned. "Stand aside."

"This time Wright's wrong," grinned Doc Daniels.

Comanche Coombs guffawed at his master's pun, but broke off short. Daniels was whipping a revolver from inside his shirt for Fant Wright had dropped a gnarled hand to his gun. Daniels and Coombs fired so close together the reports seemed joined. Razorback Kerr was a breath behind them and Wright was sagging when the third slug hit home. In his supple youth Wright had been fast on the draw but age had stiffened his muscles, slowed his reactions. His teeth gritted as he fell.

Comanche Coombs reached him in a

bound, kneeled to check up. "He's cooked, Doc! How about his horse?"

"Fetch it inside, we'll take care of everything after dark. The old goat had his nerve with him, didn't he? Well, now it will be simple."

The sun had dropped behind the rise of mighty Texas, the hinterland looming vast behind the coastal Gulf plains. A strange half-light purpled the world just before the night. Coombs went and led in Wright's saddled mustang. Razorback Kerr slouched on a bench, rolling a quirly. Doc Daniels chewed away at the pencil and his bulging eyes held a faraway expression as he lapsed into one of the queer silent moods which sometimes seized him.

The first impression given by Gus O'Toole was that of neatness and with it, efficiency. This was no lie, for O'Toole by diligent work and shrewd business acumen had raised Dillard Sherrill's Loop S ranch from practical bankruptcy to a state of solvency.

His body was strong and lithe and he looked larger than he really was. His red, crisp hair was trimmed, his chaps and blue shirt, the fresh bandanna, were clean. Sky-blue eyes gravely regarded the beholder. His Stetson was canted at the correct jaunty angle, the strap taut under a firm chin. O'Toole knew cows and horses. He knew how to conduct a ranch, which meant handling men as well as stock. The fiery hair hinted at his quick temper, but he was equally ready with a jest. He was invaluable to his employer.

The Loop S lay north of the dirt highway between Rusk and Nacogdoches. Stands of longleaf pine and other timber were properly spaced about the rolling red range. Small streams which were part of the Neches River system, furnished water.

Sherrill had fought throughout the War, had come home to find his ranch in a sad state, cattle unbranded and running wild. It had been a hard struggle for him as it had for so many of his kind. Three years ago O'Toole had come along, asking for a job. The Trail to Kansas was opening up. Sherrill had considered driving a herd north, but did not have enough men for such a long, dangerous trek. O'Toole had worked out a deal at Galveston, selling Loop S cows there for shipment to New Orleans. The run was much shorter and they had completed it in relays. This had started the ranch on the trail to success. Several clever gambles had further built up the cash reserves.

Dillard Sherrill had a righteous nature but

his forte was leadership rather than business. The rancher was the first to admit that Gus O'Toole had saved him from going under. He let O'Toole have his head, depending on the manager's ability. The War had taken something out of Sherrill.

That late Friday afternoon O'Toole dropped the reins of his black riding horse, Inky, in the Loop S yard. He unsaddled Inky, gave him a drink at the trough and turned him loose to roll in a back corral. Then he strode to the kitchen door from which wafted appetizing odors of frying beef and potatoes, of coffee coming to a boil.

The ranchhouse was low but roomy, built of native lumber. It stood above highwater mark on the largest of the creeks. In season Sherrill employed half a dozen riders. The Loop S was not a big spread for Texas but there was plenty of room.

O'Toole's silver spurs jingled pleasantly as he walked. He paused in the open doorway and looked in. A young woman, her pretty face flushed from the wood stove's heat, was cooking the evening meal. She was slender, her shining dark hair swept back and held by a red ribbon at the nape of her curving neck.

"Howdy, Esther," called O'Toole.

13

She started and looked around, her long-lashed violet eyes like stars when she smiled. Esther Sherrill was the mainstay of the household. Her mother had been an invalid for some time and Esther took care of the two young children as well as the home.

"Oh hello, Gus. I was just going to ring the bell."

"I'll do it." O'Toole seized the short, thick stick hanging by a wire outside and struck the bronze bell several sharp blows. It had a high timbre and the sound carried a long distance. When the cowboys heard it they would come running. It meant food or a call warning of danger.

In the lean-to the long board was set. The hands and family ate together here. O'Toole went in and gave Esther some help, carrying plates of steaming food to the table. Just as they finished, a smiling, mischievous little girl of eleven, Penny Sherrill, Esther's sister, bounded in, trailed by Dick who was two years younger. Penny ran to O'Toole.

"Did you fetch me the ribbon, Gus? Did you?"

"I didn't get as far as town today, Penny. But I reckon I will tomorrow, and then I'll buy one for yuh."

"Penny! Where have you been?" asked Esther sternly. "You're supposed to be here in time to set the table."

Dillard Sherrill came through from the front of the house. He had salt in his hair, and in his pointed goatee. He was a Confederate veteran and during the Battle of Virginia had lost his left arm, the shirt sleeve pinned up.

"How's it look over there, Gus?" asked the rancher as the foreman went to him.

"Good enough, boss. Found more calves than I expected."

Penny carried a tray to her mother's bedside, then returned to the kitchen to help wait on the men. Several cowpunchers trooped in, bare heads dripping from being dipped in the trough as they washed up.

"I figgered we'd head for Rusk in the mornin'," said Sherrill, as they ate the bounteous repast. "I want to see John Miller, and Esther says we're out of coffee and other stuff."

"Can I go, Dad? Can I?" cried Penny.

"No, Penny. Yuh went last time. It's Esther's turn. You stay here and take care of mother."

Next day Esther, Sherrill, Dick, and Gus O'Toole, dressed in their best, started for Rusk, where the family owned a "Sunday house", they could spend a night when they visited town. Sherrill drove the wagon while

15

O'Toole rode alongside on Inky. It was clear and warm and the holiday was welcome. O'Toole smiled at Esther, his sweetheart and she smiled back, the two young hearts lilting. The boy Dick was excited, eager for the treat.

The road slanted down into Rusk, spreading from its compact center to surrounding hills. The earth was red and sandy, broken by the creek and by patches of woods. Pulling up before a combination bakery and brewery which was famous as a refreshment stop for travelers, they bought fresh-baked gingerbread and home-made beer.

Sherrill looked up the long street. He shook his head gravely. "Never saw so many toughs around, Gus. Since the rail come, they drop off regular."

Rusk was a trading center and had done a brisk business during the War. Now the meeting of two new railroads had revived the town. Saloons and gambling houses were crowded and doing a rushing business. Buildings were going up, joining the lines of homes and stores already in place, some with false fronts, and made of local timber.

The Sunday house belonging to Sherrill stood on the outskirts south of the center. It was only a two-room cabin, just big enough to serve as a sleeping spot for the family overnight. O'Toole went with them to the place and helped open up. Esther wanted to go shopping and he left her later in the afternoon at the stores, Dick in her care. Sherrill had to see an old crony about some business and O'Toole moved over to the Dutchman's, the largest of the saloons. He went in and stood at the crowded bar. Already "Saturday Night" had begun. O'Toole looked over the bunch. As Sherrill had said, a tough element had recently descended upon Rusk, perhaps attracted by the flow of money from the brisk trade which had sprung up. O'Toole was aware that Rusk was unable to maintain a city marshal. Several incumbents had been shot or frightened off and it had become a standing joke with the rough faction that such an official could not last twenty-four hours. Most men went armed. The average individualistic Texan had an airy indifference toward anything which did not personally concern himself, and upset conditions still prevailed throughout the decade following the War.

As dark fell, a powerful man in leather and spurred boots, his Stetson pushed back on his dark head, strap loose in its butternut runner, pushed up to O'Toole and nodded.

"Yuh savvy me? My handle is Comanche

17

Coombs. Bartender! Here, set 'em up."

"Howdy," replied O'Toole politely.

Coombs paid for the round, leaning on the bar. He was swarthy with a high-bridged nose and black eyes. He must have Indian blood in him, thought O'Toole, who knew that Coombs was a tough and a dangerous customer.

After pouring long ones from the new bottle for O'Toole and himself, Comanche shoved it to a broad, squat man of Mexican strain who slouched at his other side. "Drink up, Farrizzo."

Farrizzo was a follower of Coombs. His wide, round face was enlivened by a bristling mustache and he sported velvet clothes and a peaked sombrero. He did not glance at O'Toole, but stared at his liquor.

"Price of beef up two cents, that's *bueno,* huh?" said Comanche, smacking his lips over his whiskey. "Have another. Don't be bashful, it's on me. Say, yuh work for the Loop S, don't yuh? I hear yuh're a smart operator, O'Toole. Nice spread there. I was over yore way last week."

As he listened to Comanche's small talk O'Toole tried to figure why such a character was showering him with attention. The toughs would not bother decent folks unless they had a motive such as robbery or perhaps when crazy drunk. Coombs seemed sober enough. O'Toole was shrewd and alert, seeking to pick some hint from the spiel as to why Coombs had approached him. He had no doubt that the powerful man was a rustler when it suited him.

"Yore boss come into town with you?" inquired Coombs after a time.

O'Toole nodded. The question was a direct one, and he had to answer. The center of Rusk was small enough so that Sherrill would surely be seen, and after a few more minutes the Loop S chief entered, his empty sleeve pinned up. Dillard Sherrill was accompanied by his old friend John Miller, a stout, gray-haired fellow. Sherrill saw O'Toole, waved to him and approached the bar.

Coombs and Farrizzo were squinting at Sherrill under the bright lights of the crowded saloon. O'Toole had a warning of danger, guessed it was not himself but Sherrill that Coombs was interested in. For an instant he thought the two gunhands were going to start after his chief, but this was hardly the time and place. The killing of a one-armed, peaceful citizen of Sherrill's repute, in sight of so many witnesses, would be folly even for such brash men as Coombs and his partner.

"Listen, Gus," Sherrill said, "after a drink, John and I are goin' to put on the feed bag at the Rusk House. Yuh aim to eat with Esther and Dickie?"

"Yes suh. I'll find 'em at the Sunday house."

Sherrill went to a vacant table with his crony. Coombs nudged Farrizzo, and O'Toole did not miss this although Comanche had tried to hide it. The Mexican downed his drink and eased away, leaving the saloon by the front batwings.

O'Toole did not know just how many more followers Coombs had on deck. Any of the hard-eyed men playing cards in the Annex or drinking it up along the bar could be under Comanche's orders. The manager did not like the feel of things. "They're after Sherrill," he thought. Why, he could not say. Most people would have missed the slight warnings manifested by Comanche Coombs but O'Toole had sharp intuition.

He waited, figuring Sherrill was safe in the lighted bar. When he saw that his boss was on the point of leaving, he glided quickly around Coombs, saying, "I forgot to tell Mister Sherrill somethin'. Be back pronto."

Comanche took a step after him but

O'Toole was at Sherrill's side. "Go out the back way, pick up a horse and ride home to the ranch. Don't argue, suh," he said in a low voice.

Sherrill had had plenty of military training and experience on the frontier. He hid his surprise and smiled as he nodded. "Fine. I'll see yuh later, Gus," he answered loudly.

O'Toole rejoined Coombs who had turned from the counter and was watching Sherrill. The manager was prepared to whip his Colt and cover the rough or shoot it out if he had to. Sherrill and Miller rapidly strode toward the rear exit. Farrizzo was no doubt waiting on the sidewalk, for Comanche Coombs betrayed irritation as the rancher disappeared through the back hall. O'Toole stepped in front of Coombs as the latter started after Sherrill.

"I'll buy this round, Coombs," said the manager.

The fierce black eyes glowed red at the core as Coombs braced up to O'Toole. For one reason or another Comanche decided to postpone the fight. Maybe he hoped to catch Sherrill later, and not make a public issue of it. He could not know what O'Toole had said to the rancher. Sherrill would obey, aware that O'Toole would take care of Esther and the boy, that if he made a fuss and insisted on explanations it might ruin them all.

Night had fallen and Sherrill did not need much of a start. Coombs tossed off a glass with O'Toole who narrowly observed him, ready to tangle with the breed if necessary. Then Comanche gave him a farewell grunt and swung away, leaving by the front doors.

O'Toole trailed him to the low porch. He looked up the road and saw Comanche and Farrizzo boarding their mustangs and the two moved toward the Rusk House, north of the Dutchman's. They had heard Sherrill say he was going to the hotel to eat.

O'Toole wasted no time. Coombs had plenty of confederates in the settlement, which deserved its nickname of "Six-gun Junction." He picked up Inky and hurried to the Sunday house. Esther and Dickie were there. "Can't stay, Esther," he warned. "Somethin's come up. We're goin' home. I'll hitch up the team."

Dickie was disappointed and did not hesitate to say so. "What's the matter?" asked Esther. "Is father all right?"

"So far he is and I aim to keep him that way. Get ready to leave."

In a few minutes he started them on the road back to the Loop S. Esther and Dickie could both handle reins. O'Toole lingered near the Sunday house, watching the windows and the open door. He had left a lamp burning inside on a table.

Nearly an hour passed before O'Toole glimpsed the shadowy figures around the Sunday house. They were at the windows and in the faint shaft of light the manager was sure he recognized Farrizzo for one, and Comanche Coombs for another. Disappointed at the Rusk House in hunting Sherrill, they had come here. There were at least half a dozen more armed fellows with Coombs now, and the wind brought the harsh voices to O'Toole when they realized the house was empty, their prey gone.

"Go fetch every man yuh can pick up," he heard Coombs command. "They've run for it. That cussed foreman must have smelt a rat!"

"And yuh're it," thought O'Toole.

He pulled away from the vicinity of the Sunday house, crossed the street and made the highway leading to the Loop S. It was deeply rutted, and stands of longleaf pine and other growth cast patches of black shadow across the road.

O'Toole rode slowly, turning often to listen.

Two miles out of Rusk he caught the sharp clop of a shod hoof hitting a rock.

Riders were following him on the pike and he had no doubt they were Coombs and his gunslingers. They were coming fast, at full gallop. "I'll have to slow 'em down," he decided. He must give Esther and Dickie time to reach home. Sherrill would be safe enough, on a fast horse in the darkness.

O'Toole spurred Inky along, and after a quarter mile more came to a bend where the shrubbery fringed the ditch. He turned his horse and waited, drawing a six-shooter and making ready.

He became aware of the enemy's approach, thudding of hoofs, clinking metal and creak of leather. Dark figures broke into his range of vision and O'Toole raised his gun to throw two bullets over them, close enough so they would hear the ominous shriek of metal. The sharp reports echoed in the patchy moonlight.

It proved most effective. They ripped at their reins, pulling off into the ditch and woods. Stabbing flashes marked blasting pistols as they tried to draw his fire and nail him down but he was whirling and on his way, riding hard for the next stop.

They would be slowed, would not dare rush for their goal after his attack. Playing hare and hounds, O'Toole delayed them, firing at the outlaws, then running. At every bend in the road they had to scout and feel along.

The first touch of grayness had come over the land as Gus O'Toole reached the Loop S. Sherrill was home and the wagon which had brought Esther and Dickie stood in the yard. They had just made it.

The manager sang out his warning. "Here they come, a passel with Comanche Coombs! Come on, Loop S, we got a fight on our hands!"

Cowboys rushed to him, carrying shotguns, pistols and carbines. Defense was hastily mobilized. Comanche Coombs and fifteen armed toughs came galloping up the lane. Seeing they were expected they opened fire, bullets smacking the wooden walls. Indian war-whoops and howls mingled with the explosions.

CHAPTER II
CHALLENGE

Austin, heart of Texas, basked in the balmy sunshine, which gilded the Capitol dome and warmed the shanks of legislators who had stepped outside during recess. The blue Colorado flowed gently as though it would never think of flash-flooding through its scarred, deep bed, of boiling muddy torrents into the lower reaches of its course. Westward Mount Bonnell thrust to a clear sky.

But at least one heart in the city was not at peace this lovely day. The gantlet had been flung down and in his office at Ranger headquarters Captain William McDowell felt it had been thrown straight at his head, loaded with lead besides. He sprang to answer this challenge with the alacrity of an unusually hot tempered crusader, snorting with such audible violence that for a moment the clerk in the anteroom believed a wild bull must have escaped from the cattle yards and thrust its head in the window.

Realizing it was his superior officer giving vent to his feeling, the elderly clerk murmured to himself. "Doggone, I ought to build myself a cyclone cellar for when the Cap'n feels this way. I better see where Hatfield is."

McDowell paced his floor, talking it over with himself. Once he could drive through the most dangerous, exacting jobs but age had jealously claimed its toll. He was tall and he could still shoot with the best but his joints were no longer so supple. He was chained to his desk, to paper work and the higher command, invaluable as a guiding light to the younger men who physically carried the law to Texas.

"Six-gun Junction!" he snarled. "A purty name for one of my towns. I'll six-gun 'em."

When he slammed the call bell against the wall the oldish Ranger who acted as clerk peeked around the door. "He's comin', suh. Be here in a jiffy." He ducked back fast as McDowell took a step toward him.

A soft tread sounded and a very tall young man came in. The sight of him soothed McDowell as he looked up into the gray-green eyes of Ranger Jim Hatfield, his star investigator. There were never enough Rangers available, what with budget cuts and politics.

27

Hatfield drew the hardest cases, often forced to go it alone.

Pantherish power reposed in Hatfield's long muscles. He tapered from the wide shoulders to a narrow waist where hung his twin six-shooters in supple holsters. He wore half-boots, a cowboy's clothing, Stetson pushed back on his jet-black hair. The clean bronzed face had tight jaws but a wide, good-humored mouth showed how gentle he could be with the right people. He seemed to be made of hickory and rawhide when necessary and his polished speed with Colt or other gun was unmatched. Yet it was not only the Ranger's mighty efficiency in action which had fetched him to the top. He had a keen brain to match and his strategy and tactics were those of a first-class general's. He could improvise and triumph against terrific odds.

"Here, look," growled McDowell, getting it right off his chest. "They're callin' Rusk Six-gun Junction there's so many armed bandits around. No law there! The toughs boast no city marshal can hold his job more than a day. I got specific complaints too. Fant Wright, an old-timer, shot to death and throwed in the ditch. The Loop S, belongin' to Dillard Sherrill, a veteran officer, attacked, two cowboys hurt. They tried to down Sherrill himself. Town's named after a Texas hero, General Thomas J. Rusk, one of Sam Houston's field officers. I knew Rusk, he was a great hombre. Why, he'd turn over in his grave and rise up shootin' if he could!"

Hatfield nodded and glanced over the letter written to the Rangers by Dillard Sherrill. It told of Comanche Coombs and his bullies, of the menacing conditions.

"I got an alarm out for Comanche Coombs," nodded McDowell. "The Rangers want his hide, Hatfield. He's savage as they come. Used to operate across the Pecos but he's moseyed east for a spell."

Gathering all available information, Hatfield rose and took his leave of McDowell, who felt better now he had sicked his ace on the evil-doers. McDowell watched from the open doorway while Hatfield threw a long leg over the beautiful golden sorrel waiting in the shade. Goldy was the Ranger's war horse, strong enough to carry the big man and stand the grueling pace on the trail. In the saddlebags and poncho-rolled pack Hatfield carried what spare equipment and rations he needed, and a carbine rode in its boot. He waved to McDowell as he swung off through Austin. . . .

His first halt was at a neat cottage on the

outskirts of the city. A youth of sixteen was banging away with a light carbine at a target butt set up in the back yard and Hatfield dropped rein and went around to see how he was doing.

"Howdy, Buck," he called.

Buck Robertson swung and saw his tall mentor. "Jim! I'm shore glad to see yuh!"

Buck was lean and tall, his sun-browned face freckled, his hair bleached tow color. Brown eyes danced in his head, his nose tilted up. He sported blue levis and a gray shirt, bandanna at his throat.

"School out?" asked Hatfield, smiling at Buck's exuberance.

"Yes suh. We're done for the summer. Hurrah!"

A young woman came from the kitchen door to greet the visitor. Anita Robertson, Buck's sister, was a school teacher. Hatfield had helped her and her brother when they had been set upon in a Brazos town, and they had become fast friends.

When possible the Ranger took Buck with him on his forays, teaching him Ranger lore. His sister knew it was the best possible education and training for a youth, and she was willing to let Buck travel with Hatfield though it meant anxiety for her since the work was most perilous.

The light glinted on Anita's golden hair. Her figure was exquisite, and her amber eyes smiled up at the tall man. "Come in, boys. You must eat a good meal before you leave."

When they had eaten the hearty dinner cooked by Anita they said good-by. As they came to the turn Hatfield glanced back to see her standing on the veranda, watching them. Buck frisked along on Old Heart 7, his chunky gray mustang, happy to be on the exciting jaunt.

As they rode Hatfield told his companion something about the job. "Dillard Sherrill's Loop S lies between Rusk and Nacogdoches. This Ben Coombs is wanted for outlawry in other parts, the Rangers are after the sidewinder. He's mighty ornery. . . . We could take the train over but I reckon the road's better. Should make it in two days."

They were not too many miles from Rusk. They had passed through wooded sections broken by rolling ranch lands. The red dirt pike wound through a grove of longleaf pines, with oaks and maples also visible.

"Plenty of maple sugar made in these parts," said the Ranger, who tried to instruct Buck as much as he could. "And they get turpentine from these longleaf pines. When they refine it they got rosin, what some folks

31

call naval stores. The lumber's valuable for buildin', railroad ties and cars and for ships. Cotton, cane and corn do fine. Say, what's that up yonder?"

Something lay in the ditch with swarms of insects buzzing over it. The sprawled object proved to be a dead black horse. The Ranger and Buck pulled up to stare at it. "Shot through the head," remarked Hatfield. "Leg busted and his owner had to kill him."

You could see the broken limb doubled in an unnatural way, and the officer pointed out that the rider must have been coming from the forest at a sharp clip, his animal had slipped into the deep ditch and cracked a bone. "Saddle's gone, either he toted it along or cached it. The second, I'd guess, for any hombre careless enough to come out blind at such speed would be lazy too, I reckon." The gray-green eyes gravely regarded the youth to see if Buck was paying attention. Hatfield sought to develop Buck's powers of observation by example.

They trotted on around the bend and a wooden sign warned in black letters, "Watch Out For Hogs!"

Hatfield indicated this. "That's sort of our business, ain't it?" he smiled, and Buck chuckled. Outlaws they tracked after were apt to be piggish, stealing from decent folks.

The piney woods were full of wild razor-back swine and the old boars, sharp of tusk and truculent of temper, would charge a man or a horse without a second snort.

A mile past the spot where they had seen the dead black mustang they sighted at a cross roads a little general store, all by itself. They had come upon a number of its type during the ride. It was built of native timber, of a single story with front veranda and kitchen addition. They rode to the shady side, unsaddled and hung their hulls on the log rail.

Followed by Buck, Hatfield approached the front. The door stood wide in the warm afternoon, and the shady interior was pleasantly cooler, as they stepped in. Counters and shelves were lined with dress goods, patent medicines and such wares. The square room was pungent with mingling odors of kerosene, ground coffee, harness oil, spices and cheese.

The elderly owner, in a stained canvas apron, leaned over a counter chatting with a single customer, a bulky man with rounded, beefy shoulders who turned his black-whiskered face to watch them as they entered. He had a hard look. The walnut-stocked six-shooter had that hand-polished gleam telling of habitual use while a shotgun leaned near his hairy hand. He wore leather trousers and a laced shirt, curved Stetson and runover boots with Mexican spurs stained with the red earth of the road. As soon as he saw him, Hatfield recalled the dead mustang they had passed in the ditch. No saddle was in sight, either on the veranda or in the store. "Cached it," he thought. "That was his horse."

The storekeeper's hair was white and he beamed through thick-lensed, steel-rimmed spectacles. "Good afternoon, suh," he sang out warmly. "Where yuh from and where yuh bound?"

"From west and goin' east," replied Hatfield.

The black-bearded man weighed him after giving a quick nod. Through an open door they saw a dining table and a woman of sixty who might be the owner's wife. "If yuh need to eat, ma's got plenty on the stove," invited the proprietor.

"We're hungry as a pack of wolves."

As a rule a satisfying meal could be made in such stores. As they neared the Gulf coast they had been able to purchase cove oysters and fresh fish along with crackers, cheese and coffee.

Before long they were seated at the kitchen table, waited on by the smiling woman.

Halfway through the late lunch Hatfield caught the sudden stamp of hoofs in the yard and Goldy gave a sharp whinny. He shoved back his chair and glided out the back door.

"Keep still, cuss yuh!" ordered a low but urgent voice.

The gent with the black beard was attempting to saddle Goldy without undue commotion but the sorrel did not like it. As Hatfield swung the corner the golden gelding lunged and bared his long yellow teeth at the thief, nearly pinning him to the wall.

At that instant the tough sighted the Ranger. He swore and whirled to snatch up his shotgun which he had leaned against the log rail while he sought to slap the hull on Goldy.

He had his hamlike paw on the breech and was bringing the barrel around when Hatfield, lunging fast, was upon him.

CHAPTER III
"WATCH OUT FOR HOGS!"

The Ranger's long fingers closed on the horsethief's thick wrist. He might have whipped a revolver and killed the black-bearded rough but that was not his way, nor was it the method of the Texas Rangers. The worst of outlaws was offered a chance to surrender.

Hatfield had a grip like a steel vise, the trained skill of the expert officer. He applied pressure, suddenly let go, stepping aside so the bandit lost balance from his own strainings. He ripped the shotgun loose and flung it away. The black-bearded fellow howled and struck at him with a clenched fist. The blow glanced from Hatfield's jaw, sliding over his hunched shoulder. He grabbed again and pulled the thick-bodied killer to him.

In that grizzly embrace the breath was forced from the man's lungs and his ribs crunched. He tried to bite and gouge and knee the Ranger, but swiftly the life-giving oxygen failed and his struggles abated. Hatfield then relaxed his arms, snatched the Colt from his adversary's holster and bringing up one leg rushed the gasping thief hard against the rail. The edge caught him in the small of the back, and he sank to the beaten red earth, his lungs heaving.

In those brief seconds of struggle the Ranger had not spoken. From the corner of his eye he sighted Buck coming around to give him a hand.

He waved the lad off. He had taught Buck military obedience, a vital requisite in Ranger operations.

Fear glowed in the pupils of the red eyes that bulged up at the victor. The outlaw expected death, but as the Ranger failed to pull a revolver and shoot, Blackbeard's bully's nerve surged back. When he could find the breath he snarled and spoke.

"Yah, yuh better not plug me! Comanche Coombs will strip off yore hide and nail it to the wall if yuh do, I'm a pard of his. Reckon yuh savvy that. Blackie Pyle, that's me." He pushed to a sitting position, glowering.

Hatfield watched the twisted, red-skinned face, the black beard bristling. Pyle was silent for a time, then slowly rose and

37

slapped the dust from his mussed clothing.

Blackie Pyle posed the Ranger a problem. He could not shoot a man who had quit fighting. There was no place to lock up the prisoner, and he could scarcely keep Pyle with him under guard. From information received at Austin, Comanche Coombs had taken over in these parts. It was not strange that Pyle should conclude the tall fellow was afraid of that savage, powerful band. Such as Coombs would kill anyone who dared attack members of his circle.

Blackie understood only the jungle law of night and fright and hence attributed these urges to others.

The only thing to do was to fall in with Pyle's conclusions, that the big stranger knew Blackie was a follower of Comanche Coombs. The elderly storekeeper might have warned the guests about it. "No hard feelin's," said Hatfield. "After all, yuh tried to steal my horse. I had to take away that shotgun, didn't I?"

Blackie stared up into those gray-green eyes. "Huh. Most busted my wing." He was ruffled and despite his tough front had felt the stark terror at the prodigious strength and agility of his opponent. He swung and stalked around the corner, sitting down on the porch.

Hatfield let him go. He returned to the kitchen and finished the meal. Neither Pop, the old storekeeper, nor his wife said a word about the incident. The Ranger decided they were fearful of Comanche Coombs' outlaws and hoped to stay neutral so the toughs would not descend upon them some dark night.

Blackie Pyle stayed on the veranda, they could see his burly, hunched back through the open doors. Paying up, Buck and the Ranger saddled their animals. Hatfield was alert but Pyle did not approach them or attempt again to win a new mount by seizing Goldy or Old Heart 7.

The two hit the road, picking up speed as they left the little cross roads oasis behind. The highway curved through piney woods, dark at either hand. "Watch Out For Hogs!" warned another sign. Several times they heard cracklings in the brush and savage snortings.

"Sorry we bumped into that Pyle, Buck. He's one of Comanche Coombs' pards. It can mean trouble later. He may not know yuh next time, but he'll not forget me in a hurry. I'd have been easier on him if I'd known who he was, mebbe I could have hooked into and reached Coombs quicker, but now the cuss will never forgive me.

"When yuh're on a job like this one there's always the hope yuh can work in with a passel of outlaws, but if yuh make an enemy like Blackie right off the reel it's a sight harder. We must be mighty careful around Rusk. I'll buy yuh another hat and shirt when we hit town, for Pyle didn't get much of a peek at yuh."

As the miles fell behind, fields of cotton and cane opened on either side of the road. Smoke stained the azure sky ahead and on their right ambled a yellow-watered creek, pine woods on higher reaches.

Suddenly, with no warning, a huge, grotesquely ugly razorback boar charged them from the purplish, thickly planted cane. His curving tusks were long, and sharp as daggers and he traveled with a galloping horse's speed, vicious little eyes crimson with fury.

"Get along, Buck," shouted the Ranger, pulling a Colt and firing across the hog's snout. But this only made the creature angrier. Old Heart 7 gave a tremendous bound and the boar missed but tried for Goldy, passing the sorrel's leg only inches away. His momentum carried him on several feet before he could whirl and charge again. By this time both the golden sorrel and the chunky gray were in full retreat.

"Whew!" cried Buck, glancing back. "I'd

hate to meet him without a fast horse under me. Wonder who owns him?"

"He has a nick in one ear but I'd like to see whoever put it there catch him now. Those piney rooters as they call 'em are descended from hogs, the Spaniards fetched to Texas long ago, Buck. They're shore salty."

Dusk was at hand as they topped the last rise. Below lay Rusk, spreading out from a compact center. The rays of the setting sun caught the tracks of two new railroads which had recently criss-crossed at the settlement. "There she is, Buck," said the Ranger. "Six-gun Junction."

A factory siding came from the north woods and farther on joined the east-west line. They eased their horses downhill, rumbled over the creek bridge and turned up Main Avenue. Stores, saloons, eating houses, homes were lighting up. Traders and cowboys, gamblers and others of the demi-monde showed, saddle horses and buggies at the rails separating sidewalk and road.

Saloons were filling as work ceased for the day. A mixed train of passenger coaches and cattle cars was puffing south from the junction.

"The Rusk House." Hatfield and Buck decided to put up there. They made for the hotel which offered food, drink and beds. Rubbing down the mustangs, they hung up their hulls and went through to the desk.

A prominent sign, lettered in red, confronted them:

GUESTS WITHOUT BAGGAGE PAY IN
ADVANCE AND DON'T YOU FORGET
IT!

Loud voices came from the side bar. Hatfield dug down and paid for a second-floor cubicle with two bunks in it. "We'll wash up and eat. Come on, Buck."

After they had dined Hatfield gave Buck money and told him to buy another shirt and a different kind of hat. "Meet yuh at the room later. Take a looksee for yoreself but don't horn into any trouble, savvy? From now on we'll keep apart in public."

The tall Ranger strolled around the central section. As the night advanced Rusk began to howl, and it was obvious that the tough elements were there in force, armed, swaggering gunslingers crowding the bars, coarse voices raised in boasting or drunken argument. The law was at a minimum and Hatfield saw no city marshals who might be supposed to control the riff-raff. During late hours peace-minded citizens remained indoors or walked circumspectly.

Acquainting himself with the immediate terrain, Hatfield soon learned that the biggest, noisiest and most lurid of the saloons was the Dutchman's, right smack in the middle of town on Main Avenue. Red, purple and yellow globes shed light from burning lamps, the hot smell of vaporizing kerosene mingling with the odors of humanity, stale whisky and free lunch foods.

The bar, with crystal mirrors behind it, ran down the right side of the main room, all the way from the front batwings to the rear hall exit. To the left were tables and chairs occupied by men and smiling women, with gamblers at their trade in the annex. Farther back were long counters where free lunch or heartier meals were to be had. Aproned bartenders, Mexican and Negro waiters, other employes were busy serving the customers.

The bar was packed three-deep. Rusk was certainly booming, the arrival of the rails having attracted commerce and jumped the price of city lots and surrounding rangelands. Speculators had rushed in to open shoestring offices while shady characters had hurried to the spot, ever alert for easy money.

It was nine o'clock by the round clock over the bar mirror when the Ranger entered the Dutchman's. A few slight changes had helped give him a rough aspect. He had applied two or three artistic smudges to his rugged face and tightened his chin strap. His guns rode loose and high in their holsters and he walked with an exaggerated swagger. Nobody could play an outlaw role better than Jim Hatfield who had handled plenty of the breed and knew their mannerisms. Under his high-heeled boots the damp sawdust crunched and several women entertainers watched the tall figure with melting eyes as he advanced along the great room, ducking as he came to a beam.

He stood inches above the crowd.

At a free-lunch table he paused, and a Negro made him a roast beef sandwich. A knot of heavily armed, obviously tough fellows were at the bar a few paces off and one of them sang out, "Hey, Comanche! Look, no hands!" He was clowning, gripping his glass of liquor in his teeth and throwing back his head as whisky gurgled down his throat. A crony poked him in the back ribs and the redeye spilled all over his face and shirt front. Sputtering and cursing, the drinker heard the guffaws of his comrades.

Hatfield did not see Blackie Pyle in the crew. In a low voice he asked the waiter, "Which is Comanche Coombs, boy. The one with the nose?"

"Yes suh, that's Mister Coombs." He rolled his expressive eyes. "Better not go near him, suh. He don't like bein' bothered."

The waiter sought to warn him off. Finishing his sandwich Hatfield slowly approached the group. On McDowell's Wanted circulars had been a written discription of Comanche Coombs, and this was the Ranger's man. He had a powerful body clad in range rider's clothes, leather pants tucked into spurred boots, a brown shirt and reversed red bandanna, sand-hued, huge Stetson with curving brim.

The nose bridge came out like a shelf before abruptly plunging floorward.

High cheekbones, dusky hide and black eyes spoke of Indian blood. Upcurving sideburns, a cropped mustache and overweening vanity marked the man's face. Twin Colts, gold filigree patterning the grips, rode in his holsters while a long knife snuggled at his lean ribs. Comanche was only a shade shorter than the mighty Ranger who had come for him.

There was always a certain element of

danger in prodding such a bunch. An officer might be recognized by some enemy or a drunken tough begin a quarrel which would end with gunfire.

Chapter IV
Roper

The fringe of Coombs' sycophants became aware of the tall stranger's steady pressure as he elbowed in.

"I got nothin' to lose," thought Hatfield. "And plenty to gain if I can snare this cuss first-off." He had worked out a plan and with his usual courage was putting it into effect.

"Where yuh think yuh're goin'?" snarled a red-faced bandit, forced aside by the officer.

"I aim to spiel with Mister Coombs, hombre." Hatfield dog-eyed the other who, after a moment's bristling, decided against further objection. The newcomer had a certain look which discouraged bullies.

A wide Mexican in velvet and sombrero, sporting a black handlebar mustache, nudged Comanche Coombs, who turned his head to see who was coming. A blank expression in the Coombs' dark eyes made

Hatfield certain that he did not recognize him.

"I got an important message for yuh, suh," said Hatfield easily. "But it's mighty private."

Coombs put his tongue in a leathery cheek while the others awaited the chief's reaction. Hatfield again had that sensation of a delicate balance which a hair could sway one way or the other. Such fellows often struck from caprice, at a fancied slight or just a glance they resented.

But Hatfield's voice and manner were correct and his appearance impressive. Somewhere within his dark inner consciousness Comanche Coombs made his decision. He threw down the rest of his drink. "Come on, Farrizzo. Rest of yuh boys stick here, I'll be back."

Men made way for him quickly as he strode off. Hatfield trailed Coombs while the wide Mexican brought up the rear, ready to protect his master. Farrizzo's plump brown hands swung limply close to his pistol butts.

Coombs went through a hall at the end of which they could see the kitchens. Comanche kicked in a door to his right, disclosing a private room furnished with table and chairs, a bunk, a small light turned

48

low on a stand. He did not sit down but faced the entry, watching the tall stranger enter with Farrizzo at his spurs.

"Well?" snapped Comanche.

"I just pulled in from Austin, suh," said the Ranger.

Corrugations deepened between the sulky black eyes. "Austin!"

"That's right. I heard the Texas Rangers aim to come here and tame Six-gun Junction. They mentioned yore handle for special attention."

"I'll take care of any two-bit snakes they send around," growled Comanche.

But he was impressed and affected by the warning. Few as the Rangers were in numbers they held the respect of good citizens and the fear and hatred of law-breakers. Such a man as Comanche Coombs might sneer at local officials but the Rangers meant something else.

"Who told yuh to see me?" Coombs' manner was fierce, but the tall messenger coolly stood his ground, aware that Farrizzo was at his back with ready gun.

"Nobody special. Figgered yuh'd want to know. I would. They've printed a circular with yore description plastered on it. Here." From a shirt pocket, his hand moving slowly and carefully so they would not misinterpret his action, Hatfield drew forth a soiled, folded sheet, shook it out and handed it to Coombs. It was an official "Wanted" bill, offering a reward for Comanche's capture.

Comanche shrugged. "Seen it. Where yuh figger you come in, hombre?"

Hatfield feigned to hesitate. Then he shrugged. "I might as well tell yuh, I figger I can trust yuh. On account of me the janitor in Hades has two more on his hands. One of 'em wore a silver star on a silver circle."

Coombs blinked. "Yuh shot a Texas Ranger?"

"Had to. He kept comin' at me, the fool. But I broke loose."

"Witnesses see yuh?"

"I don't think so. I'm clear, but I didn't want to run any chances so I headed this way, aimin' for New Orleans."

Comanche weighed this, his murky eyes veiling his inner emotions with an Indian's taciturnity. A Ranger killer was a marked man. On the other hand Coombs hated Rangers above everything. "How soon yuh figger they'll get here?"

"Mebbe tomorrer, mebbe next week." Hatfield gave an impression of icy efficiency, no alarm in his voice or manner. There was a know-how about him which drew Coombs as a magnet does steel.

Comanche made his decision, kicked a chair toward the visitor. "Take the load off yore feet, hombre. Farrizzo, ring for the waiter. Let's have a drink."

Soon the trio sat at the round table, consulting over a bottle. The door was shut. Hatfield maintained just the right air of respect toward a master outlaw while exhibiting his own acumen and mettle.

"First place Rangers usually go to is the local sheriff or the city marshal," he observed.

Faint sardonic amusement showed in Coombs' face. "Ain't any here. Not a cuss in town dares pin on that badge. It means he's done for inside of twenty-four hours."

"Huh." The Ranger tossed off a drink and poured another as Comanche shoved over the bottle. He considered what Coombs had said. After a time apparently had a bright idea, though he had been working up to it from the start. "If yuh had a feller you could trust as marshal it would be better, suh. He could keep yuh tipped as to what went on. Yuh'd need someone that folks don't know belongs to yore crowd."

It was a good idea, especially with the arrival of Rangers imminent. It would calm some of the better element's qualms. Comanche Coombs saw that. "How about yoreself?" he suggested, as Hatfield had expected he would. "Or are yuh in an all-fired rush to make New Orleans?"

"I could stick. Don't believe they got much description of me and I changed my rig after pullin' out of Austin. I'll know when the Rangers come. But if I take the job I'll have to put up a decent front in public. How could we work that?"

He was leading Coombs along, holding out hidden bait so the outlaw would believe he himself was doing most of the thinking. "S'pose I order a couple of my boys to act tough with yuh in the Dutchman's?" suggested Coombs. "Yuh can face 'em down and run 'em to the calaboose for the night."

"Swell! It's a deal."

"I got influence here. I'll give the order and the feller who tells the mayor what to do will see yuh're appointed. By this time tomorrer yuh'll be wearin' that tin badge. Drink up." Comanche was pleased with what he considered his own high strategy.

Blue smoke from cheroots handed around by Coombs rose slowly to the low ceiling. Music and the hum of voices, the stamp of boots came from the saloon. Comanche began what he considered a skillful cross examination of the recruit and Hatfield allowed himself to be drawn out bit by bit as to a highly imaginative bandit and rustler career he invented from the many real biographies he had become acquainted with in the course of his work. The story was faultless and Coombs was hooked.

Hatfield was especially accomplished at this type of psychological roping. Drink for drink he kept pace with Coombs and his silent Mexican lieutenant, Farrizzo. Mellowed by his own self-congratulation, boasting of his exploits to impress the new member of his organization, Comanche leaned forward across the table, lowering his voice a bit and clutching the half-consumed cigar between stubby brown fingers.

"I need a real hombre for a certain job, Hanford." That was the name Hatfield had tossed in as his own while they chatted.

"Can I help?" asked the Ranger. "If it's up my alley, count me in."

"I ain't shore. There's a ranch between here and Nacogdoches, the Loop S. Belongs to a one-armed sidewinder named Dillard Sherrill. The quicker Sherrill's pushin' up daisies, the better."

"You mean one hombre is holdin' yuh up? How about some of these fellers who are takin' yore pay, suh? Can't they get this Sherrill?"

"We tried," answered Coombs. "But Sherrill was warned and slipped us. He's got a cussed foreman named Gus O'Toole who's mighty sharp. They've set up a good defense at the ranch and beat us off. Can't get near the place now, without losin' too many men."

The recruit rolled his cigar between long fingers, staring at the rising smoke from the smouldering tip. "Someone they don't know could make it. What if a law officer rode up? Sherrill would come out to talk."

"O'Toole and the cowboys would shoot yuh after yuh plugged their boss."

"Not if it's worked right. I could use Sherrill as a shield and shoot him when I was clear, spread the news he'd resisted arrest. How strong is he outside town?"

"He's only got a few riders. There's a couple other spreads north of his we're after, but so far they ain't joined up against us. Gettin' Sherrill is mighty important."

"It could spoil our trick with the Rangers, if it set the folks here against me."

"We can cover up for a week or so. None of the Loop S dares ride to Rusk now."

"I'll do it day after tomorrer, then."

"Bueno." Coombs thumped the table with his fist. "You talk like a real man."

Hatfield was seated sideways to the door, Farrizzo on his right, Coombs facing the entry. From the edge of his eye the Ranger saw the portal open and then the black-bearded face of Blackie Pyle, the horsethief encountered at the cross roads store.

Pyle recognized him at the same instant, gave a sharp yelp and dug for his Colt.

CHAPTER V
THE DRAW

Pyle's hairy hand gripped his smooth pistol stock. His thumb joint caught the hammer, and the barrel came clear, the Colt would cock by its own weight as it rose, and all Blackie would need to do was lift his thumb. That would send a slug into the tall man sitting at the table.

Yet with the same abrupt suddenness with which he had begun his draw, Blackie Pyle quit. He froze in position, looking stupid and frightened, the pistol muzzle still pointing down at the floor.

Without shifting, without rising from his chair, the Ranger had whipped a six-shooter from an oiled, supple holster, and Blackie found himself staring at the round, unblinking death's eye of the muzzle. The unbelievable swiftness of the officer's slim hand, the astonishing coordination of muscles and brain which made such a draw possible, took away the observers' breath.

"Quit it!" snapped Comanche Coombs. "Quit it!"

Yet before he had time to speak the play was finished. No shooting had been required, with Pyle worsted. The hairy hand relaxed and the Colt dropped back into its sheath.

Not only had Hatfield acted to save his own life as Blackie Pyle went for his pistol but he realized that the way he handled the affair would weigh heavily with Comanche Coombs. Such celerity and unerring deadliness were not to be found in the run-of-the-mill gunslinger. It enhanced the recruit's value immensely in the mind of the outlaw chief.

"What's all this?" blustered Coombs. "Yuh loco or just full of redeye as usual, Blackie?"

As Hatfield only held him with the gun Pyle found his tongue. "Neither, Boss," he replied sullenly. "I had a scrap with this wild man this afternoon. He near busted all my ribs and he smeared me. He's an eyeballer."

"Yuh lie in that beard of yores, Pyle," said the Ranger severely. To Comanche he said, "This fool tried to steal my horse, when I was puttin' on the feed bag at a country store a few miles from Rusk. If that's a sample of how he goes about it I'd say he needs some lessons in his work. He told me he was a pard of yores, so I let him off."

Coombs stared sourly at Blackie and then at the Ranger, weighing what each said. Under the tall recruit's spell he wished to believe Hatfield and there were no holes as yet in the newcomer's story. "Yes suh, Blackie acted like he was takin' candy from a baby," grinned the Ranger, jeering a bit at Pyle, who would never be friendly with his conqueror. Hate bred suspicion and Blackie could not forgive the licking taken. "It was right in broad daylight with me sittin' in the kitchen. My horse won't let strangers touch him and he fussed when Blackie wanted to saddle him. I could hear it plain through the open winder and when I oozed around the corner Blackie even had his back to me and his shotgun leanin' against the wall. I didn't have to draw but got my hands on him."

Comanche Coombs made up his mind. "This hombre is workin' for me, Blackie. I'll ride the river with him. Go have a drink and forget it, savvy? And next time don't go off half-cocked."

Pyle scowled, but did not argue further. He grunted, turned on his heel and stalked off.

The crisis had passed. Coombs remarked, "He flies off the handle too easy."

"He don't seem too bright," nodded the Ranger. "He was boastin' what a tough bunch yuh had. Appears to me that ain't good policy. S'pose I'd been a lawman on my way here?"

"Yuh're right." Coombs swore. "He's dumb, that Blackie cuss. I'll give him a talkin' to."

They drank and talked further, perfecting plans for what the tall recruit was to carry out. Late in the evening Hatfield went over to the Rusk House to turn in. Buck was in bed and the officer shucked his boots and hat, hung his gunbelts on the back of a chair close to his hand, and slept.

According to schedule, the mayor, an elderly incumbent with a timid mien who was certainly not looking for any trouble with anybody, let alone such as Comanche Coombs, pinned a circular nickel-plated badge on Hatfield's shirt when the Ranger called at city hall next day. "City Marshal, Rusk, Tex." proclaimed the letters etched into the metal. "Yuh're It, mister," declared the mayor. "Yuh asked for the job so don't blame me. The city won't pay funeral expenses."

"*Gracias,* suh. But I don't reckon I'll need apply."

It had been agreed that the new marshal

59

would not hobnob with Coombs and his lieutenants in public. He was supposed to be an honest agent appointed by the administration to keep order. In the warm afternoon, Hatfield showed himself in the central section, the nickel badge shining brightly in the sunshine. Snugged in a secret pocket was his real emblem of office, the silver star on silver circle worn by Texas Rangers. Hatfield preferred to enter a troubled district incognito and line up evidence before displaying his authority.

The city marshal's office was a small cubicle next the two-cell lockup attached to the town hall. Hatfield sat around there or patrolled the streets. Buck Robertson, who had now seen Comanche Coombs, Farrizzo and others of the tough element holding Rusk, loitered in the plaza. He was to observe and keep clear of his tall friend for the time being.

Commerce occupied Rusk, freight and passenger trains pulling in and out of the junction. Wagons brought in bales of cotton, loads of sugar cane, Fuller's earth, lumber and local produce to be shipped to market. Stores were busy, citizens at work, women in voluminous bustled skirts whose hems dragged the dusty roads going to shop, children running before them or clutching their hands. Little was to be seen of the toughs during the earlier daylight hours. They made a practice of drinking and gaming into the small hours, then sleeping till late afternoon. As dusk fell over the mighty hinterland of the Lone Star State, these denizens emerged and took over.

Hatfield ate a hearty steak dinner at the Texas Lunch. He was to enter the Dutchman's just after nine o'clock, before honest folks retired to their homes. The showdown was arranged. At nine he left his office, lighted by a single lantern, and stopped to pull the rope of the bell hanging in city hall tower. Nine yanks announced the time, one of his duties through the night. Then he crossed the plaza and wide, dusty Main Avenue, entering the ornate saloon.

He had kept an eye peeled for Blackie Pyle, thinking that perhaps his enemy might take a shot at him from some hidden spot. But he had not again seen Pyle nor was Blackie in the bar. But a number of roughs, belonging to Coombs' band, were on hand. They watched him as he strolled through the large saloon, swung and pushed up for a drink at the counter.

Down the line sat Comanche Coombs himself, with the ever-present Farrizzo. Coombs was inwardly amused at the play which they had fixed up. It tickled the man's sardonic humor; and while his dark face showed no sign, it was difficult for him to keep from grinning.

Others not in the know eyed the tall newcomer. That marshal's badge pinned to the blue shirt was an invitation to death, according to experience. Timid souls carefully shied off, getting away from the marked officer.

"Who yuh shovin'?" The harsh voice rang sharply in the bar and men stopped talking, turning to see the expected fight.

The tough challenging the marshal wore leather and a "Nebraska" hat, a prominent Colt. He needed a shave and his eyes were rimmed with red. On Hatfield's other side stood a second actor, a bony outlaw with sallow hide. The first shoved Hatfield who bumped hard against the bony man.

"Why, I'll tear yuh to pieces," screamed the latter, dropping his hand to a gun.

The marshal jumped back, at the same time making a draw swift as magic. He covered the pair who looked sheepish as they stared into his pistol muzzle. "I intend to keep order in this town, boys," announced the Ranger. His voice rang loud and sure. Astounded citizens stared unbelievingly as the officer took the first round.

"You boys are goin' to the calaboose. Drunk and disorderly. Reach and march."

"Hey!" Comanche Coombs' harsh yell caused the marshal to pause and glance around although he was alert and his gun stuck on the two he had arrested. "Yuh can't take my pards."

"Careful, suh, unless yuh wish to go along," answered the Ranger coldly.

Coombs was secretly enjoying the game. The expression on the faces of those who were unaware of the arrangements was most comical. Farrizzo and Comanche stayed at their table and the tall man ran the two toughs outside and across to the lockup. He let them into a cell, passed them a bottle of liquor and deck of cards.

"Nice work, boys," he complimented. "We fooled 'em."

The sallow man chuckled and the other was laughing. "Yuh shore looked on the prod, Marshal! I could hardly keep from bustin' out laughin' right in the saloon."

Later, Hatfield went in the back way at the Dutchman's to join Coombs in the back room. Farrizzo was present as usual. Comanche slapped the tall man on the back, highly amused. They drank and talked over plans.

"I'll head for the Loop S tomorrer, suh,"

63

said Hatfield.

"*Bueno.* Want any men along?"

"Rather go it alone. They savvy yore boys and it might wreck my style. I'll down Sherrill if I see the least chance. Might have to put it off the first time, but I hope to get him right off the reel."

"Fine, fine. Drink up, Hanford."

Loop S — 1 Mile. A finger made of a branch tacked to the signboard indicated the lane turning from the road. Behind Hatfield lay Rusk, and the highway meandered on to Nacogdoches. This was range country broken by stands of timber and low hills in the background. He could see bunches of grazing cattle here and there.

The new marshal's fame had flashed through Rusk with the rapidity of a sparking powder fuse. He had run two toughs to the jail, they had paid fines in the morning, and Comanche Coombs had been faced down. When he had moved through the town streets, going for breakfast and then to saddle his sorrel, people had pointed him out, his success the chief subject of conversation. Men saluted him with the deepest respect and women watched the tall figure with admiration.

The sun was high and very hot as he

reached his destination. He had left Buck in Rusk, ordering his young comrade to keep an eye on Comanche Coombs for the time being.

Hatfield rode Goldy slowly along the winding lane, which was bordered on one side with scrub woods. On his shirt was the nickel-plated marshal's badge. He was careful to move as a peaceful man should, for from all reports the Loop S was on the prod, living on a hair-trigger.

The Loop S stood north of the dirt pike. The earth was red, the longleaf pines on the slopes dark against the hue. Small streams offered plenty of water for stock and those who dwelt there. The Ranger emerged from the trees and saw ahead the low, roomy house of native lumber, a small bunkhouse, corrals, sheds and such structures as were required by a working ranch. A faint plume of smoke came from the kitchen chimney but outside of that the place looked entirely deserted.

The ranchhouse was still twenty-five yards away when a hard voice challenged him. "Halt!"

It came from the square stable and Hatfield was aware of a rifle muzzle pinning him from a small, open side window.

"I'm a friend. Hold yore fire, suh," sang

out the Ranger.

This was the most ticklish moment. The Loop S might shoot first and ask questions afterwards.

CHAPTER VI
PUZZLE

The sun beat down on the baked yard, you could feel the savage heat. The sorrel rippled his golden hide, hoping for shade and a chance to reach the creek below. "What yuh want?" demanded the man behind the rifle. "What's yore handle? Where did yuh get that tin badge?"

"Curious, ain't yuh?" drawled Hatfield, cocking one leg as he faced the window.

"We're havin' trouble," answered the sentry. "Nobody asked yuh to come here. Never saw yuh before. Mebbe yuh're a stranger to these parts and don't savvy what's up. Now's yore chance. Turn yore horse and sashay."

Hatfield held his ground. "I want to see Dillard Sherrill."

"Yuh can't see him. He don't talk to anyone who ain't at least ninety-nine years old. I can see yuh're still just a toddler. Toddle along."

"Why don't yuh step outside so we can talk?" inquired the Ranger, ignoring the sarcasm. "I got an important message."

"It wouldn't be made of lead from Comanche Coombs, would it? That badge never fooled me." The man in the barn was agile of mind as well as of tongue. He had concluded the marshal's insignia was a ruse to work the visitor to Dillard Sherrill.

Hatfield slowly dismounted and dropped rein. He unbuckled his gunbelts and hung them from the horn. When he stepped toward the window his long hands were in plain sight.

"All right," called the hidden man. "I'll be out. Only don't forget yuh're covered from the house too."

In a few moments a young fellow came around the stable. The first impression he gave was of neat efficiency. His body was strong and lithe, his crisp red hair trimmed, clothing unusually clean and in good order. Sky-blue eyes drilled the tall Ranger. "I'm Gus O'Toole. Spit it out, what yuh got to say?" He checked some paces off, gripping the carbine at the ready.

"Yuh're Sherrill's manager, then. Yore boss mentioned yuh in his letter to the Texas Rangers."

O'Toole started as he found he was staring at a silver star on silver circle cupped in the outstretched hand. He knew what that meant. "Yuh make a collection of badges?" he inquired. "If yuh're a Ranger why yuh wearin' that tin trinket?"

"I've already gone to work in Rusk, O'Toole. I've leeched on to Comanche Coombs and aim to pull him down. He had me appointed marshal to fool folks. But I'd like to talk with Mister Sherrill."

O'Toole was still loath to endanger his employer. He hemmed and hawed and not only did he watch Hatfield but he kept shooting glances toward the woods and lanes as though he believed the tall man must have accomplices hidden nearby. He was shrewd and ever alert and the Ranger could only admire him for it. He would have acted the same way in such a situation. He began to think that Gus O'Toole would make a strong ally, and he saw he must fully gain the manager's confidence before he could reach the rancher.

"Mind if I unsaddle and let my horse go to the creek? It's mighty hot standin' out here in the sun."

"Help yoreself." O'Toole dropped the carbine butt to the ground to roll a quirly.

Hatfield saw to Goldy and O'Toole trailed him to the shady side of the stable where the Ranger sat down on an upended log and fixed a smoke. "Cap'n McDowell is chief of Rangers at Austin, O'Toole. Mister Sherrill wrote him and I'm the answer. I had luck and worked in with Coombs, yore enemy. I was appointed marshal at Rusk for two reasons. First I'm to let Coombs savvy when the Rangers pull in. Second, I'm s'posed to kill Sherrill since the outlaws haven't been able to do it."

OToole blinked. "The second is what I figgered when I saw that badge."

"Why is Coombsie so all-fired hot to down yore boss?"

O'Toole shook his handsome head, pushing back his Stetson. "It's a puzzle. I was in town with Mr. Sherrill one weekend and Coombs picked me up at the Dutchman's and pumped me. I decided he was on the boss' trail and managed to run him clear just in the nick. Since then they've come to us twice but we beat 'em off."

Hatfield's magnetic personality was exerting its spell and O'Toole found himself smiling and confiding in the visitor.

"The ranch is goin' to pot for we don't dare ride too far from home base," continued the manager. "Have to keep sentinels out nights and on guard all the while. I guess you can see Mister Sherrill. That is if

70

yuh don't mind me right behind yuh."

The Ranger nodded. "Whatever yuh say. Yuh're doin' a fine job pertectin' him, O'Toole."

"Mickey!" sang out the manager.

A waddy armed with a Sharps buffalo gun, a weapon which could do about as much damage as a small cannon, emerged from the house kitchen with such alacrity it was obvious he had been waiting there, no doubt with the heavy rifle trained on the stranger. Mickey was black-haired, debonair and young, one of the ranch's ace riders. Silently he obeyed O'Toole's hand signals, and entered the stable to take up the post covering the lane.

"Step right over to the back door, suh," invited O'Toole, politely allowing the Ranger to precede him. He was practically convinced now about Hatfield but still took no unnecessary chances.

In the roomy kitchen Hatfield sat at the board table as O'Toole desired. "Esther!" sang out O'Toole.

A slim young woman in a blue dress, her shining black hair caught up by a ribbon to match, came through the corridor and paused before them. Hatfield rose and swept off his big hat, bowing before her sex and beauty. She smiled with shy, flushed

71

pleasure at his gallantry. O'Toole said, "This here is Ranger Hatfield, Esther. He wants to see yore father." Her long-lashed violet eyes were brilliant as stars. You could see there was an understanding between the handsome manager and the pretty girl.

"Coffee?" she said. She fetched a large pot kept hot on the back of the stove, set out white china cups, a pitcher of condensed milk and a bowl of sugar. A plate of ginger cookies she had made that morning gave off a spicy aroma. After serving them they went silently back through the hall.

Drinking coffee and enjoying the cookies, Hatfield became aware of other presences. Glancing around he sighted a smiling little girl of about eleven who flirted at him with her eyes and giggled audibly. A small boy accompanied her and they were peeking at the visitor.

O'Toole pointed at them. "That's Penny and Dickie, the kids. Their mother's sick. Esther does most of the work around. Here comes the boss. He left his arm in Virginia."

Dillard Sherrill entered the kitchen, an inquiring expression on his triangular face, pointed by a graying goatee. His left sleeve was pinned up. Hatfield could tell at once that Sherrill was a sternly upright person, a man who would fight for his beliefs and principles. He was of medium height and build, wearing old but clean ranch clothing, his salted hair combed back.

As Hatfield rose to shake hands, he realized that Gus O'Toole was on edge, still alerted. O'Toole had trained himself lately to take no chances with his employer's life and the habit was too strong to discard.

The amenities seen to, Sherrill pulled up a chair and sat down for a cup of coffee. Hatfield exhibited the Ranger star and Sherrill quickly accepted him since the officer knew the contents of the letter the rancher had sent McDowell.

"Why is Comanche Coombs on yore trail, suh?" asked Hatfield, when they had talked over the complaints.

"I can't tell yuh."

"How about yore neighbors? Have the outlaws gone after 'em?"

"I guess yuh could call Fant Wright a neighbor though he'd quit ranchin', he lived in a shack this side of Rusk. I believe Coombs killed him but there's no proof. Outside of Fant, who was my old friend, there's only two, Jake Butler of the JayBee on the northwest and Art Gerdes, his brand's called the Shark, looks like a fish. We're friends enough but yuh savvy how it is. A feller hates to annoy his pards, and so far Coombs ain't jumped 'em. They'd help if I yelped for it but there's no sayin' when the bandits will attack and a rancher keeps busy day and night these days."

The Texans were fierce individualists as Hatfield knew. They did not like to cry for assistance but preferred to defend themselves.

"Yuh reckon Comanche is head man in all this?"

"As far as we savvy he is," answered Sherrill, and Gus O'Toole nodded.

"Are they rustlin' yore cattle?"

"Some, but not wholesale," said O'Toole.

The Ranger absorbed Sherrill's side of the story. For the most part the information gained was negative and did not add much to his store of facts but he sized up Sherrill and O'Toole, got the feeling of it. It was his practice to check carefully before going into action.

"I have a toehold with Coombs, suh. I'm city marshal, secretly in cahoots with the thieves, that's what Comanche believes. He expects the Rangers and is needled about it. And I made him think I was comin' here to drygulch yuh. Now, yuh can do me a big favor and mebbe cinch it with Coombs so I can rope him right."

"What's that, Ranger?"

74

"Keep out of sight entirely durin' the day for the next week. I'm goin' to report to Coombs I drilled yuh. O'Toole can send in word yuh're done for."

"I'll do it," nodded Sherrill.

"I'll send Mickey to Rusk," said O'Toole.

Hatfield shook his head. "No, O'Toole. Hold yore boys here, where they're safe. The toughs will kill any of yuh who dares poke his horse's nose into the city. Send a message some other way, mebbe someone will be passin' on the road. And in case Coombs has watchers spyin' from a distance yuh might even run off a mock funeral. Bury a box on the hill, savvy? It will look right."

"We'll do that," agreed Sherrill. "We can work it easy, can't we Gus?"

"Yes suh. But if yuh believe Coombs has men with field glasses or telescopes trained on us, what about now? They'll see yuh leave, won't they?"

"Shore. I aim to fix that." Hatfield finished with the talk and final arrangements. Sherrill and the Loop S would sit tight, the rancher hiding indoors throughout the daylight, until Hatfield contacted them again.

The tall man went out, O'Toole at his side. Hatfield whistled and the trained golden sorrel left the meadow grass by the creek and came trotting to him. "That's a beautiful horse," said O'Toole.

"Blackie Pyle thought so, too." Hatfield grinned as he told the manager of the encounter with Coombs' agent.

The Ranger saddled up. "Here we go," he said. Dillard Sherrill showed in the side yard, walking slowly around the house. Gus O'Toole turned and moved toward the stable, for Mickey, the cowboy sentry, must be tipped off to the play. There was a very good chance that Comanche Coombs had observers with telescopes or powerful glasses set on some brush-covered height.

When O'Toole had gone into the barn to warn the waddy, Hatfield waved his hand to Sherrill. He held the sorrel's reins in his left hand. Suddenly he whipped out a Colt and fired three bullets in the rancher's direction. They were well off course so Sherrill was not endangered but at any distance this could not be ascertained. Dillard Sherrill raised his one arm and gave a shrill screech, staggered around for a moment, then fell with histrionic effect.

The tall man leaped on the sorrel and pelted off toward the creek. O'Toole and Mickey rushed from the barn and threw slugs over his head, while Hatfield feigned to be shooting back at them as he made his swift escape.

When the supposed killer had crossed the stream and got away, O'Toole and Mickey hurried to the prostrate rancher's side. O'Toole knelt there, removed his hat. And Esther came from the kitchen, wringing her hands and play-acting as she flung herself on her father's body. Then O'Toole and Mickey carried the limp form inside.

"That should do it if anyone's peekin'," murmured Hatfield to the gelding, as they cut up a long, wooded slope and made for the road to Rusk.

Night had fallen when the tall man with the marshal's badge dropped rein outside city hall. His office was unlighted. A shifting shadow at the dark side of the building attracted his quick, keen eye.

"Who's that?" he demanded.

Comanche Coombs, trailed by Farrizzo, materialized from the gloom. "How did it go, Hanford?"

"Fine. I got him. He won't bother yuh any more."

"Great work." Coombs was delighted. "How did yuh work it?"

"It was a cinch. I told Sherrill I aimed to go after yuh and offered to help him. When I saw my chance I drilled him and rode off. They tried for me but they were excited and

77

they missed. Whew! I'm shore done in. Need a drink and a snooze."

"Yuh've saved me a passel of trouble and I'd have lost a bunch of men smashin' that Loop S. Now we can start on the others."

"The others?"

"Yeah, there's a couple more ranches, the JayBee and Shark."

"What's the game, Comanche? Yuh after all the ranchers around here?"

"Go have yore drink and sleep. See yuh tomorrer." Coombs evaded his question.

Hatfield unsaddled Goldy at the Rusk House and took care of his horse. Then he went up the open back stairs to the second floor where their room was. Buck was already in, waiting for him.

"What luck?" asked the youth.

Hatfield gave him a quick account of it. Buck had news, too. "I watched Coombs all afternoon and evenin'. After supper he rode to a big square house on the north edge of town and went in for an hour. I found out it belongs to an hombre named Porter Daniels, they call him 'Doc.' "

"Yeah? What's his game?"

"I don't savvy yet. But he seems important."

" 'Daniels.' I'll ask around about him." There was a chance that Coombs was working under somebody's direction and this might be it.

Hatfield slept late, rose and washed up, ate breakfast in solitary state at the Texas Lunch. He strolled over to the city hall and put his feet up on the desk, slouching back in the marshal's swivel chair, as he smoked and figured on his next move.

Near noon he saw from the open door, among other vehicles on the road from the creek bridge, a slow-moving cart packed with cotton bales coming along Main Avenue. It was driven by an ancient Negro in blue overalls and ventilated slouch hat, an old fellow with white hair and wrinkled face. The cart was drawn by a long-eared, sleepy mule.

The driver brought his team to the bare area before the building, slowly climbed down and dropped anchor, a stone attached to a frayed length of rope. He swept off his battered hat at the open door.

"Howdy, Uncle," sang out the Ranger genially.

"Howdy, suh. Are yuh the policeman?"

"That's me."

"I got tidin's, suh. Mister Sherrill out at the Loop S was shot dead yesterday."

"*Gracias,* Uncle. Do me a favor. Take this four bits for yore trouble and go over to the

79

Dutchman's. Tell the barkeep just what yuh told me."

"Yes, suh."

The messenger creaked back to his seat and drove across the plaza, stopping at the saloon into which Hatfield had seen Comanche Coombs go a short while before. . . .

At dark Hatfield lighted the oil lamp on the desk. He had hardly finished when somebody banged on the open door and the Ranger swung to confront a red-faced, blunt looking man of forty, in a black suit, stringtie and narrow-brimmed felt hat. He had the look of a successful businessman, thought Hatfield. He wore no gun in sight but he might have had one hidden in a shoulder holster under his coat. His hair was dark, his pink cheeks shaven smooth, body wide at shoulders and waist.

"You call yourself the law here?" he snapped, his eyes sparking at the tall fellow with the marshal's star pinned to his shirt. He wasted no time on preliminary greetings.

"Yes suh. I'm Marshal Hanford." Hatfield was curious about the caller, waiting so he might catalogue the stranger.

"Do you know that Dillard Sherrill has been killed?" snarled the blunt visitor.

"Yes. But the Loop S ain't in my jurisdic-

80

tion, mister. I'm town marshal."

"Town marshal! Have you the slightest idea what goes on around here or did Daniels and Coombs hire you?"

Things were looking up, thought the Ranger. He felt he had found someone who might prove of value in bracing the tough element. Doc Daniels was the man to whom Buck had trailed Comanche Coombs, and the bristling stranger seemed to know something about the inner workings of the ring.

But as he considered how he could draw out the information, his alert ear caught the cluck-cluck of a cocking six-shooter. Hatfield gave what was supposed to be a warning grimace and the blunt fellow hastily swung to confront Comanche Coombs, backed by Farrizzo, Coombs stepped in, his pistol drawn.

CHAPTER VII
MEET THE CHIEF

The Ranger watched carefully, determined to check Coombs if it came to shooting. The blunt man was alarmed but it was not the panicky fright of a coward. Rather he showed a natural healthy respect for the ready weapon in the hand of the notorious killer. His manner under the gun commended him to Hatfield. Anyone with the slightest sense would have kept quiet and not made an overt move which would further infuriate the savage breed.

"What yuh doin' here, Dunn?" demanded Coombs hotly. "Ain't yuh satisfied?"

"Of course, of course." Dunn offered the marshal a quick, appealing glance that was almost devoid of hope.

"What's he been spillin', Hanford?" asked Comanche.

"Nothin' much," answered the Ranger. "He just got here and was passin' the time of day."

A glint sparked Dunn's alert eyes. He was grateful for the lie. He took a chance. "Somebody picked my pocket in the saloon and I came over to complain."

"Huh. I'll do any complainin' there is to do. Yore train pulls out in five minutes. Be on it. And remember what yuh were told. It wouldn't take two bits for me to put a slug right through yore gizzard."

In the distance sounded a train whistle, *"Whoo, whoo!"* It was coming from the east toward the junction. Comanche Coombs gave Dunn a shove toward the door. "See he makes it, Farrizzo. Let him have it if he don't behave."

Coombs was putting on a special show to frighten Dunn who wisely kept his mouth shut and quickly left the office, Farrizzo silently after him.

Comanche turned and winked at Hatfield. "That's the way to handle such sidewinders. He didn't say anything, much, huh?"

"Nope. Who is he? I never spotted the cuss before."

"Oh, just a business deal. You got to keep the screws on them hombres or they'll steal yore pants right off yore legs." Coombs took a chair and stretched himself, rolling a quirly. He had brought a pint flask along and set it on the desk. "Help yoreself. You got Sherrill shore enough, Hanford. They sent in word. I took yore say-so for it but I'm glad to be certain. Yuh might only have wounded him."

"Not through the head and heart," grunted the Ranger.

The "killing" of Dillard Sherrill had swept away what slight reservations Comanche Coombs might have retained as to his new agent. Such a clever, successful henchman was not to be picked off every prickly pear bush. While Coombs held his air of superiority as leader and the one who issued the orders, he was ready to relax with Hatfield and trusted him to the hilt.

They heard the train puff to a stop, the screech of hand brakes ringing through Rusk. Then the engine slowly began its westward run, picking up speed outside the junction, and soon Farrizzo rejoined them.

"Yuh put him on?" asked Comanche.

"Si." Farrizzo patted his Colt. He took a bench seat along the bare wall.

A flurry of pistol shots and wild yells rose from the Dutchman's. Hatfield jumped to his feet. "I better hustle over there, Comanche. Yuh want me to keep order, don't yuh?"

"Go to it. Some of the boys must be

whoopin' it up."

Coombs trailed the tall man as Hatfield galloped across the plaza and went up on the Dutchman's porch, looking over the swinging doors. Some of Comanche's followers were in their cups and shooting at the mirror and hanging lamps. The Ranger plunged in.

"Cut it out!" he bellowed, his voice rising over the din. "I'll run yuh all in."

The rioters, who had been quarreling among themselves, turned on the marshal. Hostile glares fixed him but Comanche had given the word that he was one of the bunch. And the tall man had a look which discouraged even the toughest from facing him down. They quit shooting, some going to the bar, others heading for tables, and the crowd closed in again with the fuss over.

Hatfield went outside. He saw Coombs and Farrizzo climbing aboard their saddled mustangs and paused to see where they might be bound. They walked their animals up the edge of the plaza, chatting together in Spanish. Hatfield slid up the sidewalk, keeping to the awning shadow. He had been watching Coombs, hoping to learn more of the killer's connections and had a hunch that Comanche might be going to make a report now. A couple of blocks up the commons ended and Hatfield ducked under the hitchrail and walked across the avenue, purposely showing himself.

"Hi, Hanford," sang out Coombs. "Yuh put down that fuss pronto."

The Ranger stepped over, looking up at his supposed boss as Comanche reined in his big horse. "Yeah, just some of the fellers with a skinful. Let's go back to the office and polish off that bottle."

"Later. I got to see somebody." But Coombs hesitated, studying the rugged face. "Come along, it ain't far. I want yuh to meet my *amigo.* He's a real high-grade operator." There was quiet pride in his voice. He was showing off to Hatfield, and he also wanted to exhibit his new ace.

"Bueno." Hatfield took hold of a stirrup strap and moved along. As he had hoped, Coombs turned in at the gate of the square mansion, blazing with lights, which Buck had said belonged to Porter Daniels. A sign at the entrance told who lived here.

Coombs got down and dropped rein. "Stick here, Farrizzo. Come on, Hanford. Don't talk too much, just act natural. Leave it to me."

He rapped on the front door and soon a bolt slipped back and a man opened up, staring out at them. "Is Doc around?" asked Coombs.

"Who's that?" parried the other, indicating Hatfield. He had a hard look. He wore slippers on his feet, black pants, and his white shirt bulged from a gun carried under it.

"He's aces. Tell Doc I'm here."

The guard disappeared down the hall but soon beckoned to them. The rangy Coombs led Hatfield to a large room with elegant furnishings. Bottles of liquor and boxes of cigars stood on a handy table while two men sat facing one another before a stone fireplace.

"Well, Comanche?"

"Howdy, Doc. There's no doubt about Sherrill."

Doc Daniels nodded. He stared at the tall fellow, remaining in the roomy chair. His body was wide and heavy, his beefy neck crimson over a flat collar with a black silk tie carelessly knotted. Grease plastered down the thin brown hair and his brow bulged like a jutting balcony. Two pale-pink lines, scarcely visible in the gap of a rat-trap mouth, served as lips.

But Hatfield sensed his strength, as brutal a power as Comanche Coombs' yet shrewder and more ruthlessly sweeping.

Doc Daniels considered himself cleverer than others and perhaps he was right.

Daniels' crony was thin and bony. His wiry hair was clipped short and stood straight up. He had on comfortable, dark clothing and owned sharp features, ears rising to a tip. He was hunched as though from a sore back, the shoulder blades humped through his shirt. He reminded the Ranger instantly of the old razorback boar who had charged them on the road to Rusk. Comanche pointed at him, saying for Hatfield's benefit, "Razorback George Kerr. Best metal man in the Southwest, Hanford."

Daniels gave an impatient twitch. The bulging eyes did not shift from Hatfield. "I thought I told you not to fetch your men here, Coombs. I'm not eager to have everybody and his brother know we're connected."

"Nobody saw us, it's dark, suh," answered Comanche. He seemed desirous of pleasing Doc Daniels and there was almost a sycophant's note in his usually harsh voice. "Yuh can thank this baby for gettin' Sherrill. It's all confirmed, the Loop S sent in the word. I told yuh I'd set Hanford up as marshal, we're on the watch for Rangers. And just now Dunn went to the office to make a complaint."

Daniels swore. "Why, the hound! I thought he looked a bit shifty when I told him off this evenin'. What did you do?"

"Throwed a jolt into him, and Farrizzo put him on his train."

"H'm. I'll see to him later."

Daniels was apparently satisfied with his study of the brilliant new operator discovered by Comanche Coombs. He waved a pudgy hand toward the liquor tray. "Help yourselves, boys," he invited grandly.

Razorback Kerr was interesting, too, though obviously a follower of Doc Daniels. Hatfield decided that Kerr was actually proud of his nickname for the man kept his hair cut like hog bristles. The Ranger had bumped into others who did their best to live up to such descriptive titles.

As Coombs poured drinks and passed the cigars to Hatfield, Daniels took a pencil from over an ear and placed it between his teeth. He chewed at the end for a time and the bulging orbs glazed. He was immersed in secret fantasies, far removed from there.

Coombs sank into a comfortable chair, a glass in one brown hand and cheroot in the other.

"Yes suh," boasted Comanche. "The minute I spotted Hanford I says to myself, 'This hombre is all wool and a yard wide.'

He's got the nerve of a brass mule and I never see a feller could draw as fast, outside of myself. He rode right up to the Loop S behind that tin badge, bluffed his way to Sherrill and downed him. Then he busted clear."

Doc Daniels gripped the pencil in his teeth. If he heard anything he did not show it. Hatfield had an eerie sensation, his flesh crept in the chief's presence, as it might have before a loathsome rattlesnake about to strike. Razorback Kerr grunted now and then as he listened to Coombs patting himself on the back. The metal man had little to say for himself.

With a violent start Doc Daniels returned to the present, focusing his gaze on the tall recruit. "Coombs tells me you shot a Texas Ranger, Hanford. That's dangerous play!"

"Yes suh, it is," agreed Hatfield conciliatingly. "But nobody saw me and I pulled out of Austin the same night. I like workin' for yuh and Comanche mighty well, Mister Daniels."

Comanche Coombs was entirely sold on the tall man and to justify himself and prove his point kept booming Hatfield's stock. He had the air of a wise teacher shoving forward a star pupil. And Doc Daniels was also impressed although he was master of the

90

deadly gunslingers.

"I'll have plenty of work for you boys," said Daniels, as they talked. "You don't set up an outfit like mine without runnin' into some opposition. That's expected. Business is business. Before I'm through I'll show Texas what a real operator looks like."

"Yuh shore will, Chief," cried Coombs. "Say, this liquor goes down smooth, don't it, Hanford?"

"Best I ever tasted," agreed Hatfield.

"It should be," shrugged Daniels. "That's the finest Kentucky bourbon money can buy, I have it shipped here by express. Look here, Commanche. Tomorrow night I'm givin' a dinner for some important customers from out of town. Come around after dark, fetch Farrizzo and stick in the kitchen. No rough stuff, understand, without direct orders from me. You're to stay reasonably sober. Marshal, you show up too, at nine o'clock. Mingle in with us but keep it quiet."

"Yes suh, that's fine," said Coombs. "Wait till yuh get a mouthful of the grub Doc serves up, Hanford." He smacked his lips. "Doc, yuh should have seen Dunn when I stepped in behind him with a cocked hog-leg. He turned white as bleached alkali, didn't he, Hanford?"

But Doc Daniels was staring straight

ahead. The prominent eyes had again filmed over as he lapsed into the strange, silent mood when he failed to hear or to see what was before him. It betrayed the fact that Daniels was entirely uninterested in anybody but himself, his ego swollen and dominant. He cared nothing for others except as they might affect him. After a while he jumped, blinked and nodded.

"All right. See you boys tomorrow evenin'. Remember, I'm the doctor." He waved them away.

They threw down their drinks and smoking the fine Cuban cigars, took their leave.

"He's the real stuff, ain't he?" said Comanche, as they started back to the center. "I could kick myself when I think of all the years I've spent chasin' off a few moth-eaten cows or riskin' my neck takin' a few dollars from some farmer on the road. Doc says that in six months we'll be so rich we can retire. That's for me. I'm goin' to buy me a villa on the coast near Tampico and furnish it with the prettiest senoritas and the best rum they got."

"It sounds great." Hatfield gripped the stirrup strap as they slowly moved down Main Avenue toward the plaza. "And I can see Doc Daniels is the real Peruvian mustard. But where's all this cash comin' from?"

Comanche Coombs shook his head. "Leave it to us. Daniels is the doctor like he says. All yuh need do is foller orders, Hanford."

Strains of piano and fiddle music, hoarse shouts and the stamp of feet came from the saloons. At the freight siding a switching engine was shunting cattle cars back and forth, ready for loading in front of the roomy pens east of the city.

Comanche and Farrizzo entered the Dutchman's and the marshal looped up and down the street for a time before retiring to his office to think things over.

As he emerged from the Texas Lunch after breakfast, Hatfield sighted Razorback Kerr on a skinny brown nag, riding from Doc Daniels' toward the heights west of the settlement. The hunched back of the metal man was most evident now and Kerr most surely had the aspect of the beast for which he had been nicknamed.

The Ranger hurried to the stables behind the Rusk House and slapped his hull on Goldy. As he rode across the plaza he was just in time to see Razorback Kerr, who had crossed the creek, disappear in a lane screened by stands of longleaf pines covering the adjacent hills.

"Here goes," he murmured. He was most curious about Daniels' crony. Kerr might supply the answer to the riddle puzzling the officer, who was eager to discover the chief's motive. Once he learned this, many loose ends should tie up and he could plan his counters.

The sandy, red dirt of the winding road through the pines deadened the hoofbeats of the sorrel. The way led to a long, roomy structure obviously a factory of some sort. Hammers were banging and the clang of metal rang out as well. Kerr's horse stood in the yard with the mounts and wagons of the workmen who were busy inside.

As Hatfield came up, Razorback Kerr stepped from the open main doorway, confronting him. His spine was bent, his bony figure slanting forward. He had a pistol in the belt strapped to his lean waist.

His bristled head was bare and his tipped ears, small, fierce eyes combined to give the aspect of a rangy hog.

For a moment Hatfield felt Razorback's hostile glare, wondered if Kerr suspected him.

Chapter VIII
Party

The tall officer grinned and slid a long leg over, jumping lightly down. He took care not to turn his back to Kerr.

"Yuh're up early, Razorback."

"So are you," grunted Kerr.

"I seen yuh pass through town and thought I'd say howdy. This yore outfit? It's quite a place. I ain't been up here before, been too busy straightenin' things out for Comanche."

"Huh," Kerr seemed alert.

Past Razorback the Ranger could see through open entries into an office recently floored and decorated, beyond this a long factory in which furnaces and other equipment were being installed. New brick smokestacks were rising, masons very busy at the job. The single track of a siding ran from the far end through the woods toward the east-west line which it would join without crossing the creek. Hatfield remembered having crossed it on the pike.

"Mighty interestin', yes suh," declared the Ranger. "How's Doc Daniels this mornin'?"

"He was still sleepin' when I left. So yuh savvy about plants, do yuh?"

"I know as much about 'em as a hog does about a sidesaddle," answered the Ranger cheerfully. "Still I'm always ready to learn. What yuh aim to turn out here?"

"All sorts of things." Kerr measured the curious visitor.

Razorback backed up and Hatfield pushed inside. The banging hammers on metal made their ears ring, and one had to shout to make himself heard over the din. The Ranger poked his nose into corners. Razorback Kerr evaded direct queries and Hatfield had to draw his own conclusions, depending on the knowledge he had gained while he had studied mining engineering before joining the Rangers.

Not wishing to prod the taciturn Kerr too far and aware he was not welcome there, Hatfield soon took his leave. He rode back to the town hall and ensconced himself in his small office. "I got an idea, anyway," he mused as he smoked.

The day was quiet. He sighted Buck Robertson several times but they stayed apart. Comanche Coombs, Farrizzo and others of

96

the wild bunch showed in the late afternoon, and when dark fell Hatfield rode up to Doc Daniels' mansion. The party had already started. Lights blazed in all the downstairs rooms, there were lanterns strung in the front yard.

Hatfield dropped rein in the side driveway and started toward the kitchen door. He could look through the windows into a large dining room where the guests were already at dinner, a dozen strangers, who had the look of business people, with Daniels in fine clothing, Razorback Kerr and a couple more of Daniels' domestic circle at the long table. Wine was flowing and fancy dishes were served by Negro attendants.

Hatfield was admitted and showed himself in the wide connecting doors between the kitchen wing and dining room. Daniels beckoned to him, and pointed to a vacant chair. "Boys, there's Marshal Hanford, the law in town," introduced Daniels, and for a moment all eyes turned on the big fellow.

There was plenty to eat and the Ranger did not waste any time stoking up. The food was delicious and he enjoyed the meal, listening to the talk. Some of it was shop, about ships, railroads, the ever expanding industries of the Lone Star empire. The young man next to the officer chatted pleasantly with him. After a time Hatfield learned he represented a company which sold barbed wire. "I reckon the time will soon come when the open range will be busted up into closed pastures," nodded the buyer.

Comanche Coombs and Farrizzo had arrived and were in the rear of the mansion, eating and drinking as they waited, on tap if they should be needed.

But there was no call for the tough arm of the chief's organization. Some of the guests grew tipsy and loud, but they were not the type to go wild. After dinner they broke up into small groups. Doc Daniels consulted with one after another in his adjoining study. They were signing up, what seemed to be order blanks and contracts. Hatfield managed to get a peek at a couple spread out on Daniels' flat-topped desk, when he wandered in to speak to his boss.

A man around fifty, with temples touched by gray, was saying, "Remember, Mister Daniels, the agreement is void if not fulfilled by the expiration date."

"Yes, yes," nodded Daniels. "That's all written down here."

"I just wanted to make sure you understood."

The party broke up around two A.M.

Some slept at Daniels' while the overflow was driven to the Rusk House. Next morning they departed in various directions as trains pulled in to the junction.

Hatfield was late arriving at the marshal's office. He had hardly opened up when Razorback Kerr rode to the door astraddle his ancient mount and signaled him to come outside. "Howdy, Hanford. Be on the westbound express, it leaves in fifteen minutes."

"Shore. What goes on?"

Kerr's shrewd, piggish little eyes fixed his. "Yuh'll catch that train, Hanford. This is a direct order from Doc Daniels."

Hatfield shrugged. "*Bueno.* I'll be there, suh." He was not certain whether Kerr retained some suspicion of him or whether it was just the crabbed Razorback's usual manner. Kerr pulled rein and rode off, going toward the spacious plant.

Hatfield had just time to contact Buck Robertson. "Stick here and keep an eye on things, Buck. I'll be back."

The westbound came puffing in, clouds of smoke belching from its bell stack, showering everything with cinders. Hatfield swung on the back platform and walked through the smoker. Comanche Coombs and Farrizzo were already seated and the breed

99

winked at him as he passed in the narrow aisle. He counted two dozen more toughs, members of the breed's bunch. In the parlor car was Doc Daniels, with four of his personal bodyguard.

For three hours the huffy little train shoved its cowcatcher nose in a generally western direction. It stopped here and there to discharge or pick up passengers, express and mail, taking its time about it all. Basket venders offered fruit, cakes and beer enroute. Loud-mouthed but harmless drunks, crying babies in the arms of flushed mothers, and the rural populations gathered at every station furnished some excitement. The armed gunhands played cards or drank, some napped, jerked violently awake when the hand brakes were applied.

In the forenoon the train arrived at Waco and Hatfield left it with Comanche Coombs, Doc Daniels and the rest. The town lay in the wide, fertile valley of the *Rio de los Brazos de Dios,* River of the Arms of God, otherwise the Brazos. Hatfield well knew the lively, rapidly growing city. It lay in its big green bowl rimmed by low hills of the Balcones Escarpment, cut in two by the muddy river. Rich bottom lands grew the best cotton and other crops and the railroads had jumped Waco's stock. False-fronted saloons, old cattle trails showed along with new industrial plants. A suspension bridge had replaced the old ferry and as it was the only bridge within many miles, Waco had grown in importance with startling speed. From a dignified, live-oak shaded village she had become a rip-roaring town, and great herds of cattle, wagons laden with cotton, wheat, coal and hides, long freighting trains, lumbered across the bridge. Cowboys and buffalo hunters, gamblers and other elements flocked here for amusement and trade. Hatfield's business had brought him to Waco more than once.

Word was passed along they were to meet at the Judge's, an oasis in Rat Row as the riverbank slums were called, after dark. Hatfield found himself attached to Comanche Coombs and Farrizzo. He could not shake off his supposed employer without arousing suspicion or hurting Coombs' delicate feelings, so he tagged along as they made a round of gambling establishments and other hot spots. They ate supper together and then repaired to the Judge's. Here the rest of the tough bunch collected.

Doc Daniels was not there but Coombs

led his forces to a nearby livery stable where saddle mounts were hired. They rode a mile north of the center and Daniels was waiting for them on a road corner, took the lead. They trailed along to a large private house set off in its planted grounds. Doc Daniels dismounted under the porte-cochère. "Comanche, Hanford, Farrizzo, Ike, Jack, with me. Rest of you stick here. If I call, rush the doors and come shootin'."

Daniels stepped up and banged the brass knocker. A Negro butler opened the door and Daniels pushed him aside, Coombs, the Ranger and the picked crew shoving in after their chief.

"Where's Mister Dunn?" demanded Daniels. His eyes had a fierce glint and he kept one hand in his side pocket.

A man hurried from a door down the hall. He stopped short as he saw Daniels and the others coming at him. It was the red-faced blunt stranger who had come to Hatfield's office one night to complain, back in Rusk.

Daniels halted a few paces from Dunn, glaring at him. "I had your wire, Dunn, and here I am. We'll talk it over." Doc waved a yellow sheet with his left hand but kept his right in his gun pocket. "Well, ain't you goin' to ask us in? Where's your hospitality?" The cold grin came over the chief's features.

Dunn gulped. He backed up and Daniels crowded him into the living room. A slim, pretty woman with dark hair, two young children, were in there. Daniels bowed.

"Sorry, I didn't know there were ladies present. Better send Mrs. Dunn away so we can talk business."

The woman was frightened. Her husband frowned and gave a warning shake of his head and she gathered up her little ones and fled. Doc Daniels again mockingly bowed low as she passed him, hurrying upstairs. Comanche Coombs and the Ranger joined the two in the salon.

Daniels shook a crumpled yellow paper under Dunn's nose. "I'm here to show you what's what, once and for all, Dunn!" Evidently Dunn had wired Daniels, breaking some engagement forced on the businessman during Dunn's visit to Rusk.

"Let me at the sidewinder, Doc," growled Comanche Coombs.

But Daniels needed no assistance. His hand shot out and caught Dunn's throat. He shook Dunn violently, displaying great physical strength, hurled him against the wall and followed up, kicking Dunn as the latter slumped to the carpet. Hatfield pushed in, ready to prevent Daniels from killing his victim, no matter what the cost. He managed to shoulder the chief aside on the pretext of helping beat up Dunn.

"All right, Hanford, that's enough," snapped Daniels, eyes bulging and nostrils flared. "That's just a sample, Dunn. I've brought an army along and aim to have this out tonight. I'll clean out your whole crowd if need be. Sit down at your desk there and write messages, tellin' your associates to come here at once!"

Dunn's cheeks had turned shades redder. He was furious but knew it would mean death to resist. He staggered to his desk and began writing several notes as Daniels dictated. Comanche Coombs swaggered around, poured a drink from the decanter.

"Comanche!" ordered Daniels. "See these are delivered right away. Take the butler along, he'll know where to go."

"Yes suh." Coombs hurried away. The Ranger remained, watching, determined to save Dunn's life if it came to that. Daniels ranted at the blunt man, threatened him, hinted at what might befall Dunn's family.

In less than an hour five more men, Dunn's friends, were collected in the living room. Ringed by armed, tough killers, Doc Daniels told them off. "You'll ship me all the coal I need at the price offered or you won't ship another lump! If one of you drags in local or state law to interfere with me, the whole bunch will be responsible. I'll guarantee you won't testify against me. Business is business, and this is it!" He shook with rage, bull neck flattened on a celluloid collar, glaring at his victims. His brown hair stuck to his ill-shapen skull. There was ruthless power in Doc Daniels.

Dunn was still leader of the opposition despite the beating he had received. "We can't make a dollar a ton at your price, Daniels," he said sullenly.

Daniels stepped in, dealt Dunn a vicious slap in the face. Comanche Coombs, Farrizzo and other toughs who had drifted in seized their gun butts, ready to shoot, and Hatfield tensed.

But Dunn subsided. "I'm the doctor," declared Daniels. "This ain't an argument. I'm givin' the orders. Supply me with fuel or you don't supply anybody."

A white-haired man with a fragile look, the eldest of Dunn's colleague, said quickly, "Angus, we must accept."

Angus Dunn crouched in the armchair, trembling with pent-up anger. Yet he knew Daniels would kill him at the drop of a hat. There was no doubt as to the chief's savagery. It was a choice of surrender or death and Dunn capitulated.

"Any more trouble from this end and we'll be back," warned Daniels. "Next time you'll get no choice. Start shippin' tomorrow."

Hatfield breathed with relief as they rode away. At least no killing had occurred and he hoped to gain the upper hand in time to check Daniels' mad career. A late train took them to Rusk, most of the men sleeping on the way.

Hatfield took a chair behind Daniels and Coombs, who were riding together in the almost deserted car. "We've got to start production, Coombs," said Daniels. "No more time to waste. My contracts have time clauses, they're signed and sealed and we must deliver. With Sherrill out of the picture I'll soon have the Loop S and can get goin'. The other ranches should fall more easily."

Dawn grayed the eastern horizon as they alighted at Rusk. Nobody much was around as yet and the weary crew departed to find sleeping places. Hatfield went to his room at the Rusk House. Buck was asleep on the cot and jumped awake.

"Jim! Glad yuh're back. Say, Sis is here!"

"Anita? What's up?" The Ranger was astonished to hear that Buck's pretty sister had come to Rusk.

"She's got an important message from

Cap'n McDowell, Jim. Shall I wake her up?"

"Let her sleep a while longer, then we'll see her."

The settlement was bustling with activity when the Ranger awoke from his nap. Buck led him to a room down the hall where the youth knocked, softly calling, "It's Buck, Sis!"

Anita replied and soon the two entered. Anita smiled up at Hatfield, her amber eyes fresh as stars. She wore a starched blue dress and her golden hair curled about her soft shoulders. "I'm so happy to see you boys. I always worry when Buck and you are away."

"Mighty fine yuh're here," said the Ranger.

She had word from Austin. "Captain Bill asked me to fetch it direct to you, Jim."

Hatfield read McDowell's note. *How you making out, Ranger? This looks like it's hooked to what goes on around Rusk.* The enclosure was an urgent letter of complaint: *Please keep this secret for it will mean death to us if it becomes known we have called on the law for aid. Porter Daniels, whose head-quarters is in Rusk, commands a powerful band of killers under Comanche Ben Coombs. We are forced to deliver coal to Daniels at very low price or be shot . . .* This was signed *Angus Dunn* and had originated in Waco.

"Dunn sent this before Daniels paid him that call last evenin'," mused Hatfield. "No wonder Dunn looked sick. If Doc ever finds he yelped to the Rangers he'll rip his hide off!"

Shortly after, Anita met Hatfield downstairs. Buck kept away in public, doing his observation job for the Ranger. The two went to the Texas Lunch for breakfast. While they were dining Comanche Coombs came along the sidewalk and paused at the plateglass front window, looking in. He waved to Hatfield and then came inside, taking off his Stetson and smirking at the beautiful girl. Comanche was deeply impressed by Anita, that was obvious.

Hatfield introduced Comanche. "Doc wants to see yuh, Hanford," said Coombs casually. "He's up at the factory. Got a job for yuh."

"*Bueno.* I'll be right along, Comanche."

"I'll wait and have a cup of coffee with yuh." Coombs pulled out a chair and sat down, watching Anita.

When they had finished the meal they left Anita at the Rusk House and picking up their horses, rode to the long building on the pine-clad heights. Hatfield believed Daniels must have another strongarm task, perhaps to dispose of ranchers north of the Loop S.

Outside the plant he dismounted and dropped the golden sorrel's rein. Coombs followed, politely holding the door so the tall man could enter first. The connecting door into the main factory was shut. At the new desk sat Doc Daniels and Razorback Kerr. Kerr had not been on the Waco jaunt, this was the first time Hatfield had seen him since Razorback had dropped the order he was to catch the train.

Farrizzo and three picked toughs of Comanche's crew lounged around, smoking.

"Good mornin', Hanford," said Doc Daniels cheerfully. "You look bright-eyed today. Enjoy the trip?"

"Yes suh. It was good sport."

"Yuh ought to see the young lady he was havin' breakfast with, Doc." Comanche Coombs' voice was soft. "Prettiest little gal in the county-o!"

"Have a seat," invited Daniels. "Drink, smoke?"

"*Gracias.*" Hatfield took a chair and accepted a cheroot from the box held out by Doc Daniels, who then touched a silver call bell. As the bell tinkled the inside door came

109

open and in stepped Blackie Pyle, the be-whiskered road agent with whom Hatfield had tangled on his way to Rusk.

It gave the Ranger a start to see Blackie for he had practically forgotten this enemy in the rush of events. But he hid his emotions, giving a short nod to Pyle. Inwardly he made ready for Blackie gave the show away. He looked too eager, too pleased with himself and bursting with tidings. The Ranger, trained to dangerous situations, felt that he had stepped into a baited trap.

They were all staring at him now. Comanche Coombs' entire manner had changed, the breed had done a fine job of dissembling as he led the tall officer to the slaughter.

CHAPTER IX
EXPOSED

They were all ready for him. Daniels had taken command of the play. So far nothing out of the ordinary had been said but Hatfield was an old hand at such games. Without turning his head or betraying himself he swiftly figured what his chance of escape might be. Blackie blocked the door into the shop. Coombs slouched at the other exit. Three gunhands were craning eagerly forward on a bench at his right while Doc Daniels and Razorback Kerr were behind the desk at his other hand. The two windows on either side of the entrance were closed.

"We've run into an extraordinary situation, Hanford," purred Doc Daniels. "Blackie's seen a ghost. Tell him, Pyle."

Blackie was all primed. He burst out, "Shore. I been hidden not far from the Loop S, watchin'. Had the most powerful field glasses I could get and trained on the ranch. Yesterday mornin' I see Dillard Sherrill at an open window!"

"Yuh're a liar, Pyle," shrugged Hatfield coldly. "Yuh had too much redeye. Sherrill is dead."

The tall man's voice was contemptuous. He knew that Blackie loathed and feared him. For a moment he felt he might be able to bluff this out. Calmly he went on. "Blackie has it in for me, yuh savvy that, gents. He's been after my hide since I beat him up on the road. He's lying his ears off to put me in the pot." He glowered at Pyle who trembled even though he had so many allies around.

"Better watch him," warned Blackie. "He's quicker than chain lightnin', I tell yuh!"

Doc Daniels intervened as the Ranger bristled at Pyle. Blackie recoiled, his sharp high heel grinding down on Farrizzo's toe and the broad Mexican swore.

"Take it easy, Hanford! We're aware Pyle might lie to drag you down. Wouldn't take just his word for it. Go ahead, Razorback."

Kerr spoke in his dry voice. "While yuh were all away yesterday Blackie come floggin' in. He told me he'd glimpsed Sherrill at a window. I hardly believed him, for after all word had been sent Sherrill was done for. But I rode out with Pyle and watched through the afternoon."

"A kid, I guess it was Sherrill's boy was throwed off a bucker in the back corral. Sherrill himself rushed outside to pick him up. I had the glasses trained on the yard and I know Sherrill, one arm and all. Never had anything against yuh, Hanford, only a feelin' I couldn't explain that yuh weren't quite one of us."

"Yuh made a real big-time fool of me, Hanford," drawled Comanche Coombs. Little muscles twitched in the savage breed's high-boned cheeks, in his turkey neck. "When I think how I stood up for yuh and took yuh in out of the cold world, I could fill yuh with slugs yuh cussed eyeballer!"

"Hold it, Coombsie," frowned Daniels.

The breed subsided, fuming about it. Red fire burned in the pupils of his dark eyes and his hand itched to draw. The admiration he had felt for the supposed ace had soured inside him, turning to bitter bile. He felt particularly aggrieved since it was he who had brought Hatfield into the fold.

It was all over. The Ranger could hardly make them believe both Pyle and Kerr were lying.

"The reason you ain't dead is we're interested in findin' out what your real game is," went on Doc Daniels smoothly. "If Sherrill's still kickin', then you must be in cahoots with him for the ranch to have sent a message sayin' he was dead. Who employs you?"

Hatfield shrugged. "I stopped at the Loop S and asked Sherrill for a job. He told me yuh were on his trail and I offered to see what I could do."

"He's a root-toot-tootin' little gem of a liar," snorted Comanche Coombs. "Just as long as a snake and drags the ground when he walks!"

"Take his guns and search him, Coombsie," commanded Daniels. He picked up a pistol lying under a sheet of paper on the desk before him.

The previous afternoon, Gus O'Toole had been working and helping stand guard at the Loop S. He had been holding his cowboys close to home base since he dared not risk having them cut off by the enemy. He was aware that the ranch was suffering from neglect, that cattle would stray and the range was wide open to marauders, but this could not be remedied at the moment.

Dillard Sherrill had been staying indoors during the daylight hours as requested by Jim Hatfield. O'Toole had sent in word by a passing cart driver that his boss had been shot dead.

Both the manager and Sherrill kept hoping they would hear from their tall ally, the Texas Ranger who had come to assist them.

Hardly had they staged the fake burial on the hill over the creek when a lawyer from Rusk had appeared and put in an offer to buy the ranch. O'Toole had sent him away with a promise to think it over.

Penny and Dickie Sherrill were playing around as usual. Penny was always into mischief. She could ride like a cowboy and so could Dickie although they were forbidden to mount certain outlaw horses kept in a special corral well to the rear of the stable.

The sun slanted in against the windows of the ranch house, reflecting brilliant light from the glass. Dillard Sherrill sat back from an open window, looking out. He was bored with staying indoors and wanted to get out and work but had obeyed the Ranger's wishes.

O'Toole had a hammer and can of nails. He whistled as he mended a couple of cracked rails around the main horse corral. He was thinking about Esther, his sweetheart. Some day this terrible trouble would be over and done with. He hoped to build a home for her when they were married. He had picked a site not far away for he knew that Sherrill could not spare him, he must stay there and run the Loop S for the family. As O'Toole recalled the pleasant, wooded hillside northwest of the ranch, he glanced that way.

A scintillating flash from the height blinded him for an instant. Then it ceased.

O'Toole straightened up and lines showed in his bronzed forehead. "Why, that was sun on glass. I wonder who's up there?" Then he remembered. "I reckon the Ranger's right. They're spyin' on us!"

The two younger children, Penny and Dickie, made a good deal of noise as a rule while playing. Their voices usually did not disturb O'Toole but now they were yelling with unusual excitement.

"Hey, Gus, look, look!" Dickie was calling to him in a high-pitched screech of delight. His words seemed jolted from him and as O'Toole swung to stare, he saw why.

Dickie Sherrill, on a shaggy-hided, bullet-headed roan, worst outlaw on the place and scheduled for sale either to a rodeo or the glue factory, shot from around the barn. Behind him, riding a half-tamed bronc she handled with superb skill, came Penny, hitting the crazy outlaw with a length of rope to make him move faster.

Dickie was laughing, enjoying his role as a

buster. The roan crowhopped, whirled, but the boy stuck to him like a postage stamp.

"Jump off, Dickie! Jump off," howled O'Toole, starting to run toward the bucker.

They had roped the roan and slipped a hair hackamore on him so Dickie could try some control over the beast. The outlaw's glaring, rolling eyes, his foaming mouth, showed he was mad with fury, blind to everything except to throw off the burden on his shaggy back.

Suddenly, in his crazy gyrations, he changed ends, hit a soft spot and lost balance, either purposely or by accident. He crashed heavily on his side, the dust rolling up in a billow and hiding Dickie from O'Toole's horrified eyes. The manager for a few moments did not know whether Dickie was underneath or not. His breath surged through his lungs as he rushed in. The outlaw roan was up, kicking out viciously. Dickie lay unmoving on the ground.

"Get out of here," snarled O'Toole, slashing at the roan with the hammer handle, and the mustang shied off, running away from the yard.

Penny slid off her horse and stared at her prostrate brother. "Is he hurt?" she gasped.

O'Toole was not sure yet whether the heavy weight had crushed the boy. He

117

stooped and knelt beside Dickie, his heart in his mouth. Relief flooded through him as he found that the little fellow was only stunned, already coming back to consciousness.

"Is he dead? What is it?" Dillard Sherrill, in a parental panic when he had seen his son hurled off the outlaw, had forgotten everything else and rushed out of the house to Dickie's side.

They picked Dickie up. He had a lump on his forehead and scratches but no serious wounds. He was so light and without stirrups to catch his toes, he had been flung clear. "Get in the house, Penny," ordered Sherrill sternly. "You know yuh're not s'posed to ride those outlaws! I ought to paddle yuh."

O'Toole carried Dickie to the kitchen where Esther bathed his head with warm water. When the excitement died down the manager remembered the tell-tale flash from the hill.

This was a jolt. He had a quick comprehension and could draw shrewd deductions. "Shucks! If they were watchin' they'd have seen the boss rush out when Dickie was throwed."

It was a nasty slip and the longer Gus O'Toole considered it the worse it loomed.

He knew that Jim Hatfield was risking his life working in with Comanche Coombs. The main trick used to set the Ranger with Coombs was to make the killers believe the tall man had slain Dillard Sherrill. Sherrill alive meant death for the investigator from Austin.

O'Toole loaded his carbine and dropped spare shells in his pockets, checked his six-shooters. He drew Sherrill aside in the house and spoke in a low voice so Esther would not overhear and be alarmed. "I'm goin' over and check on that roundtop hill, Boss. I believe Coombs has spies up there. If they spotted yuh it will mean hair in the butter for Ranger Hatfield."

"Dog it," exclaimed Sherrill contritely. "I shouldn't have gone off half-cocked, but when I saw Dickie go under I thought he'd busted his neck."

O'Toole went out and saddled his black gelding, Inky. He was too clever to ride straight toward his objective for the enemy might still be watching. He moved eastward, in which direction lay Nacgodoches, the creek and Rusk on the west. Half a mile from the house he came to a feeder brook along which grew a line of timber and behind this he could work north.

Hidden from the sight of anyone on that

roundtop, O'Toole took great pains working back to it once he was beyond the eminence. Stands of timber, the contours of the range, helped screen him. When he reached the top of the hill he dropped rein and sneaked up through the brush on foot, his carbine cocked at the ready.

But whoever had been there had left. He found where they had been lying up, pressed shapes in the dry grass, crunched cigaret butts, remains of cold meals and such sign. They had not been gone long for on the western slope long, slender stems of elastic grass were still slowly returning to position, the trails of two men obvious to a trained eye.

O'Toole had brought field glasses, standard equipment for such as he. Some dust in the west attracted him and he focused the glasses on it. Two riders were trotting their horses across the rolling land, headed at a long diagonal for the road to Rusk. As O'Toole studied the figures, one horseman looked back over a shoulder, and the black blotch of his bearded face showed.

The manager felt that his worst fears were justified. "They spied Sherrill and they're goin' to report!" he muttered.

He picked up Inky and galloped home. Consulting with Sherrill, he told what he had discovered. It was late, the sun enlarged and ruby red as it sank across the creek. "Only thing is for me to head for Rusk, Boss!"

"They'll fill yuh full of lead, Gus."

"I'll have to chance it. I ought to make it before mornin' tomorrow and mebbe I can warn Hatfield before it's too late."

O'Toole had a snack and said good-by to Esther and his friends. He would not take any of the boys along for the Loop S needed every available defender and he believed he would have a better chance of snaking through alone. He borrowed a long Mexican serape and a sombrero, rolling them at his cantle, in case he should need a disguise.

Esther had been told what was going on. She stood in the yard, watching until he was out of sight. At the last bend O'Toole turned to wave. Anxious as she was about him she had not tried to dissuade him from going since she knew he must do his duty and a brave man would not flinch.

While the light lasted he rode very cautiously, sometimes leaving the highway to check up on blind turns and other suspicious points. He held no illusions as to the enemy, knowing that any of Comanche Coombs' numerous gunhands would be delighted to shoot him on sight. It would do Hatfield no good if O'Toole died.

Night fell over the vast land and O'Toole had to substitute his ears for his eyes. A chunk of moon was rising and silver light touched the red road but the shadows were black. He paused now and again to listen, as a faint breeze rustled dry leaves. Once he heard horsemen coming toward him, the clop-clop of shod hoofs, voices as they called back and forth. Hastily he drew off the way, got down and held Inky's soft snout so the black gelding would not whinny as the other animals passed. He could not tell whether they were outlaws or not.

It was late when he sighted Rusk's yellow glow. Far off a freight train whistled in the night. Rusk lay in a shallow depression, hills hemming in the town. On the other side of the bowl, O'Toole was aware there was a new railway spur, and he could make out the winding line of the creek. For the most part homes were darkened, the inhabitants asleep, but the saloons were lighted and men showed in the glow of the center.

"Now for it," muttered O'Toole. He dared not ride Inky into Rusk for such men as Coombs commanded would certainly be about at this time.

The manager unsaddled Inky and picketed him so he might graze. He hid his hull, slipped the voluminous black cape over his shoulders and strapped on the peaked Mexican sombrero. At least this changed his silhouette. On foot he moved downhill but kept away from the red road.

He knew that the Ranger had a room at the Rusk House, for Hatfield had so informed him when the officer had visited the Loop S. The office next the city jail was shut, no light on. Bit by bit, O'Toole edged toward the hotel, staying out of the shafts from doors and windows.

The lobby looked deserted save for a sleepy clerk behind the desk. The bar adjoining the hotel was occupied but the Dutchman's was the only saloon filled with customers. Raucous noise issued from it. O'Toole knew it was used as a club by the bandits and he avoided it.

O'Toole took a chance and slipped into the Rusk House, going to the desk. "Is the marshal here?" he asked.

Then he realized someone was sitting in a leather chair on the far side of the counter. The man turned around and stared at O'Toole's figure, the manager turning his face away. The fellow half hidden in the chair was a gunslinger, a foe with whom the Loop S had tangled. O'Toole recognized him at once.

"Marshal Hanford's out of town," said the clerk, answering O'Toole. "Want to leave a message?"

"No, *gracias,* senor."

"Hey, what yuh want with the marshal?" The tough left his seat and came around the counter.

But O'Toole was scuttling off, swinging through the door. The gunslinger started after him. "Stop," he ordered, but the manager made it, jumped aside and ran.

"Cuss it, if Hatfield wasn't in the soup I'd put him there if that hombre recognized me," thought O'Toole, kicking himself for having missed Coombs' agent by the desk. The outlaw drew a pistol and hunted for the Mexican figure. O'Toole ducked into the first opening and galloped full-tilt for the back road.

It took a few minutes to shake off the pursuer. The manager hastily left the center for he knew the bandit would have plenty of friends to enlist in a search. He hid in a deserted shed behind a grocer's at the north end. Through a wide crack he could watch a section of Main Avenue, and saw armed men riding up and down as though hunting somebody.

O'Toole had risen at five o'clock that morning. He was tired out and closed his eyes, back against the wooden shed wall, just for a quick nap.

When he awoke with a violent start, the light was up, the morning well along, Rusk bustling. He checked up, and then left his hiding-place, keeping to the back streets as he returned to the hotel. He kept the sombrero pulled down, the cape hiding his shape. Suddenly he sighted Hatfield, walking with a pretty young woman along Main Avenue.

CHAPTER X
TANGLE

Galvanized to action, O'Toole trotted through the passage. He reached the sidewalk in time to see Hatfield enter the Texas Lunch with the girl. But as he was about to make tracks for the place, Comanche Coombs appeared, sauntering along. Some armed toughs stood on the Dutchman's porch, watching everything that went on.

Coombs peered in at the big window and then went into the restaurant. O'Toole had to wait. They would cut him down from the Dutchman's before he could get to the door. After a while Hatfield, Coombs and the beautiful, golden-haired woman emerged, the two men apparently on the best of terms. O'Toole watched for a chance to sift out Hatfield alone.

The two tall figures, Colts in oiled holsters, escorted the girl to the Rusk House. Next, Comanche and the Ranger rode off, crossed the creek bridge and disappeared along a trail into a patch of woods. At this, armed outlaws streamed from the Dutchman's, climbed on saddled mounts, to follow. "That ain't good," decided O'Toole. From where he stood it looked just like a trap. Plainly Hatfield had no idea of his peril.

O'Toole must gamble. The bandits had started off, the van crossing the bridge. He hotfooted it along the covered walk to the Rusk House, ducked into the hotel. The woman was going upstairs and O'Toole trailed her. He overtook her around the turn into the hall.

"Ma'am, I got to speak to yuh!" He was breathless.

She swung quickly, her amber eyes alarmed. She licked her full red lip. "Who told you to speak to me, sir? I've never seen you before."

O'Toole had forgotten how he must look. His usually neat clothes were covered by the disreputable cape, the sombrero was pulled to his eyebrows. He needed a shave and his face and hands were smudged.

Then a hard pistol butt was rammed into his back ribs and despair gritted his teeth.

"Reach!" ordered a determined voice behind him.

O'Toole's hands rose, it would mean

death to resist. "Face the wall and lean there," went on the voice, and O'Toole complied.

"Don't shoot him, Buck," said the girl quickly.

His captor was feeling for his gun, jerked it free from the holster. O'Toole thought of whirling but the odds were too high against him and the woman would probably be hurt in the crush.

"Who are yuh?" demanded the tall, lean youth whom O'Toole could glimpse from the corner of his eye. He had on Levis, a blue shirt and battered Stetson. Tow hair showed above a bony face with narrowed brown eyes. "I s'pose yuh ride for Comanche."

"No I don't," snapped O'Toole shortly, chagrined to realize the victor was only a lad, sixteen years or a bit more.

"Loop S," muttered Buck.

He glanced at the neat brand sign of the home ranch which O'Toole had carved in the walnut stock of his six-shooter. "Say, yuh from Sherrill's?"

O'Toole hesitated. It would give him away but as soon as any of Coombs' men saw him they would know who he was. "That's right," he growled. "I'm Gus O'Toole, and yuh might as well savvy."

"O'Toole! Yuh're the manager," cried the youth, his manner and tone changing. "We're pards of Hatfield's, O'Toole. Yuh can trust us. He told me about yuh. How come yuh're in town this mornin'?"

"Can I turn around?"

"Here, take yore gun back!" urged Buck, thrusting the six-shooter into O'Toole's hand.

The manager swung.

"She's my sister," went on the lad. "Tell me, is there somethin' wrong, O'Toole?"

"Plenty! The outlaws spied Sherrill when he run outside. They've just lured the Ranger up to that factory to kill him!"

The breath hissed in Buck's teeth. Anita gave a small cry, her face stricken by alarm. "Come on," said Buck. "Let's get goin', O'Toole!" He ran lightly to the stairs, the manager at his heels.

In the street they looked hastily around yet both knew that before they could possibly muster aid it would be too late. Not far off stood a ranch wagon with oak-plank sides. Two strong looking chestnut geldings were hitched to it and the owner had gone inside the general store. "That's it, Buck!" said O'Toole, ducking under the railing and vaulting into the open body.

Buck did not need to be told twice. He

was right with the manager. "I'll handle the ribbons, O'Toole! They don't know me. Lie down flat and hold on."

The chestnut horses shied but Buck Robertson had an expert touch. He seized the whip from its socket and judiciously applied it, the team starting off with a jerking bound, the wheels shrieking and grinding at the sharp turn. The two-foot oak sides kept O'Toole from behind flung out and Buck had braced his booted feet, plastered to the narrow seat up front.

Up on the west slope, the tail end of Coombs' bunch disappeared among the trees. With horrific sounds the long wagon followed the powerful surge of the rushing chestnut geldings, Buck cutting across the end of the plaza straight for the bridge. The iron-rimmed wheels slugged the loose boards, making them rumble like thunder, then they were across and pulling hard up the hill.

In the office Jim Hatfield felt the icy fingers of doom reaching for his throat. Comanche Coombs, who was behind him and blocking the door, was shifting at Doc Daniels' command, coming to take the Ranger's pistols. He would also find the silver star on silver circle which would identify the tall man's calling.

Daniels cocked the gun he had kept hidden under a paper.

"I'll lay a thousand gold to a stale doughnut he's a Texas Ranger," observed Daniels. "Sometimes they bore in like this before makin' arrests."

"Yuh've hit the nail on the head, Doc!" So furious was Comanche Coombs that his teeth ground audibly. He permitted himself the intense pleasure of violently slapping Hatfield, his horn-hard right hand smacking against the Ranger's cheek and the side of his neck. It stung frightfully, the delicate nerves below the ear crying out against the blow.

But it also offered the tiniest element of hope to the desperate Hatfield. It placed Comanche, told he was off balance and his gun hand busy. It was an excuse for the tall officer to shift without drawing instant lead from all directions. He did not muff this wild breath of time offered by sneering fate.

With the pantherish speed of which he alone was capable, Hatfield threw himself back with all his weight. He was seated and this tipped over the chair, the back of which caught Coombs and doubled him up. The Ranger's long arms were reaching back and he got hold of Comanche and as they went

131

down in a stunning crash, Doc Daniels fired.

The bullet bored into the floor a foot from the struggling men, fighting like two wildcats. Daniels realized he could not shoot Hatfield without hitting his field chief. Farrizzo and Blackie, the others were drawing, starting to help Coombs. Doc Daniels jumped up, blocking Razorback Kerr for the moment.

Hatfield put all his power into a roll, banging Comanche's head against the edge of the doorway. He was aware that Coombs' grip relaxed and he broke free, Colt flying to his hand as he came up on one knee. His swift eye pictured Farrizzo, Coombs' silent Mexican crony, about to make the kill. The Ranger's Colt roared in the confined space. Farrizzo's pistol exploded but the bullet struck short. The broad figure staggered against Blackie Pyle, who began screeching. Pyle knew the tall man's terrific speed, and in his panic flung himself flat, groveling beside the desk.

The Ranger was nearly outside. Doc Daniels was next for he was cool as he took aim. Hatfield let go another bullet yet even as he raised his thumb off the hammer he felt tearing metal along his folded thigh. His slug cut a noisy furrow across the flat desk top. Jagged splinters appeared in its wake and it must have burned Daniels for he screamed and fell over on Razorback Kerr, upsetting him. The two disappeared behind the desk.

Quick bullets rattled the slower gunhands. The slashing Colt barrel connected with Comanche Coombs' temple, the sharp sight bringing the blood, knocking the breed to the floor.

Now Hatfield was out of the room. But his left leg was useless, trousers ripped, wound spurting. He rose but could stand only on one foot. Not far away stood the golden sorrel, but he was beyond that open doorway. The Ranger's cursing enemies were rapidly pulling themselves together, to drill him from the office.

The shock, the violent exertion, kept the breath burning in Hatfield's heaving lungs.

"After him! He's hit," roared Doc Daniels.

Hatfield swung to hop to the end of the building, hoping he might whistle over Goldy. Then the cool gray-green eyes sighted the riders pelting at him. They were Comanche Coombs' killers, whooping it up as they spurred in.

CHAPTER XI
FLIGHT

Gun up, the hammer spur under his thumb joint, the gallant Ranger prepared to go down fighting. He had to struggle for every ounce of remaining power, for the wound was rapidly sapping his strength. He braced himself with left hand to the wall, bit his lip hard, dancing spots threatening to blind him.

And yet even as he saw the end of it all, Hatfield was puzzled. The charge had slowed, strangely enough. The toughs were pulling around, turning in their saddles. One of Coombs' men stuck head and shoulders out the office door, seeking to pin him. He spared a shot which sent the killer jerking back out of sight.

A heavy rumbling and confused shouts came from the wood road leading to Daniels' plant. The half-wild mustangs stampeded at the unusual noises, some rearing and bucking, others bolting into the pine woods and nearly brushing their riders from their seats.

Up the line came a long ranch wagon with two-foot high plank sides, drawn by two plunging, foam-flecked brown horses. Braced in the seat was Buck Robertson, yelling at the top of his voice and plying the whip. The wheels bounced and jolted high on protruding rocks and uneven spots, the thundering vehicle traveling at break-neck speed.

Hatfield held on by a final effort, the lights nearly out. The wagon swept up, Buck ripping the chestnut geldings around with violent strength. Gus O'Toole bobbed from the body and caught Hatfield's shoulder. "Come on, come on, hop in," shrieked the excited manager.

Hatfield pushed up with his unhurt leg. He fell against the plank side. O'Toole's strong grip and the Ranger's own desperate fingers clutching at the edge kept him from being hurled under the grinding wheels for the maddened horses refused to pull up, only slowing as they swung.

O'Toole leaned way out, nearly yanked from the wagon by the big officer's weight. He took fair hold with both hands, sticking with his knees and waist against the side. Hatfield tried to pull upward and then the

Ranger balanced on the top and O'Toole rolled him over and fell on him as the wagon whirled off around the building.

They were slewed to the far side, heads banging against the hard oak but the uprights held them in. Buck let the chestnuts run for it. They narrowly missed being hung up on a pile of lumber as Buck pulled the reins. The wagon tipped far over and again Hatfield and O'Toole changed corners, slung around like sacks of meal.

"Come on, Goldy! Come on, boy!" bellowed Buck. He gave shrill whistles imitating Hatfield's call.

There was no road at the far end of the factory, only the new railroad spur to the east-west line. Without hesitation Buck took to it for this was the only way out for a vehicle. The shod wheels clumped with vicious emphasis on every tie, for there was little ballast between them.

Doc Daniels was massing for the pursuit, roaring orders as the gunslingers regained control over their bolting horses and came to the office door. Bullets sped after the wagon but Buck had a start and kept going. Horsemen spurred on their trail.

They came to the point where the spur crossed the highway and Buck swung eastward toward Rusk, not far below in the creek valley. O'Toole, gun ready, fired at several of Coombs' cronies who merged from the woods near the spot where the beaten road entered the pine woods.

They flashed past, rolling down the hill, Buck aware they had only a few breaths to spare. "Is he hurt much Gus?" called the youth.

O'Toole stared at the Ranger, crumpled in the wagon. The muscles of the rugged face were taut, the cords standing out. The manager could see the bleeding wound through the bullet-ripped chaps. "I'm all right." But Hatfield's voice was only a whisper.

O'Toole crawled to his side. He took off his bandanna, seeking to make some sort of rough bandage to check the flow of blood. Behind them galloped a golden shape, Hatfield's mighty sorrel following his friend.

They thundered across the creek bridge and swerved to the plaza, hitting Main Avenue. "Where's yore horse, cowboy?" shouted Buck to O'Toole. "These babies are plumb tuckered!" The geldings were heaving from their violent efforts.

"He's hid east of town."

The horses drawing the wagon were glad to pull up as Buck threw all his weight into checking them. They stopped not far from the Rusk House. Anita Robertson stood on the porch, watching with the deepest anxiety as her brother and Hatfield showed. There were citizens around, curiously staring. The heavy gunfire and hubbub from the west hillside had been heard in the settlement, and streams of avenging outlaws were coming after the trio.

"Get yore horse, Buck," ordered Gus O'Toole. "I'll borrow a nag, and put the Ranger in his saddle."

Buck jumped over the side, landing in the dirt, and trotted around to the hotel stables. O'Toole reached up to give the wounded officer a hand, easing the jolt for Hatfield. The Ranger could stand on one leg. His nerve held him up, the rugged face was set and drawn.

The golden sorrel came in to sniff and nuzzle at Hatfield and stood quiet as O'Toole boosted the tall man into the saddle. A bullet shrieked past them and slashed a chunk of wood from a thick post helping support the sunawnings over the sidewalk. Others kicked up spurts of dust. Some of Comanche Coombs' crew, still around the Dutchman's, were opening up on them. There was not much time, for the main bunch roared after the running three.

Hatfield's slim hand fumbled at his shirt

front. He brought forth his silver star on silver circle, emblem of the Texas Rangers, pinned it on. A heavy, middle-aged man in a ten-gallon hat, leather pants and vest, came hurrying at them from the Rusk House.

"Say, who told yuh yuh could take that wagon!" he yelled furiously, face crimson.

"Sorry, mister! Oh, howdy, Butler! Say it was life or death for us. And yuh better get out of town pronto. That passel of killers will gun yuh like they did us." O'Toole said to Hatfield, "Ranger, this is Jake Butler, owner of the JayBee, our neighbor. Ranger Hatfield, from Austin, suh."

Butler stared up at the grim officer and the light glinted on the star.

"O'Toole's right, Mister Butler. Coombs and Daniels aim to finish off Gerdes and you. No time to talk now, though. Fetch as many fightin' men as yuh can, and bring Gerdes too. Yuh better meet us at the Loop S soon as possible."

Buck came whirling his horse out of the side lane, whooping it up. Bullets were hunting them and Jake Butler was convinced. The rancher turned to duck for it, while the three rode off, cut through and made for the road out of town.

■ ■ ■ ■

Comanche Coombs and his gunslingers were coming. The rangy breed was in command, hoping to bring down O'Toole and the Ranger. Buck and the Ranger rode ahead. O'Toole had made a hurried transfer to Inky, leaving behind the saddle horse borrowed to get out of Rusk.

They were beating east by south on the dirt highway between Rusk and Nacogdoches, keeping ahead of the crush. Now and again shots would be fired at the long range. But with jolting animals under them aim was difficult. Goldy, Inky and Old Heart 7 were superior to the ordinary mustang and unless there was a slip they should be able to stay out front. Single riders surging out on fast runners were discouraged by the shrieking slugs thrown back by the dogged three.

"Yuh feelin' any better, Jim?" inquired Buck, worried about his friend.

"Yes, Buck. You and O'Toole done a neat job pickin' me up."

Buck was delighted, a word of praise from his tall mentor meant more to him than anything else.

The first stunning shock was wearing off

as Hatfield regained his breath. As he rode he had tied on a stronger bandage to check the worst of the bleeding, though the jagged flesh wound in his side still oozed. He knew that he must have rest, warm drinks and food, but his excellent physical condition and his determined spirit sustained him.

The sun was high and hot as they made time eastward for the Loop S, keeping to the beaten, winding red road.

The pace had to slow for no horse could maintain a gallop for so many miles. They came down to a trot, then to a walk as the final lap faced them. Comanche Coombs and many of his toughs were still trailing, but some had dropped out of the race and all were tuckered. At bends in the road and where woods grew, they would be screened for a while from the enemy's sight.

Hatfield had time to think things over during the long ride. Doc Daniels was now thoroughly aroused. "I reckon he'll really throw everything he's got at us," he concluded. "Wish I'd had more time to convert Butler." He was not sure that the JayBee owner realized the gravity of the situation, not only for his neighbor Sherrill, but for his own and Gerdes' ranches. The handful of fighters that Dillard Sherrill could muster could not hold long against a reinforced, determined attack.

The Ranger was racking his brains as to where he might obtain the necessary strength to check Daniels and Comanche Coombs, to check them and then counter-strike to defeat the enemy.

Dusty and frayed out, he was glad as Goldy's hoofs echoed on the planks of the narrow bridge across Stonybrook, the creek which furnished the Loop S' main water supply. A curve behind them and the piney woods skirting the way hid them from their foes.

"Buck!"

"Yeah, Ranger?" The youth grinned at him. Buck had stood the run well. He could recuperate quickly from strain and weari-ness.

"How do yuh feel?"

"Fine, Jim."

"Do yuh think yuh could reach Nacogdo-ches? I want yuh to send a telegram for me. If yuh stop at the ranch it may prove too late. I figger they'll hem us in till they can fetch up more gunhands."

"I can make it," nodded Buck.

Hatfield had a piece of scrap paper, a pencil stub in his shirt pockets. He rested the paper on the smooth curve of his saddle and wrote out a short message which he passed to Buck Robertson. "Send this soon as yuh get to Nacogdoches. Then wait there for the reply, savvy?"

"Yes suh."

"Here we are, home!" cried Gus O'Toole, eagerly pushing forward. The brand sign, Loop S, nailed to the trunk of an ancient pine, marked the ranch lane.

Buck raised his hand and cantered on southeast. He made the next turn as Hatfield and O'Toole waited off the red highway, watching. Before long Comanche Coombs and several armed toughs appeared, having crossed the creek bridge. Coombs was riding carefully, screened by his followers. He was aware the Loop S was close at hand.

Hatfield shouted to attract their attention and hold it, for he wished to give Buck a start. Both O'Toole and the Ranger opened fire with their Colts and Coombs' men scattered, spurring into the woods. More and more of the toughs came up, and hoarse commands, blind metal stinging in the leaves, reached the officer and his friend.

"I guess that did it, O'Toole. Let's go."

Before the snaking killers could work around through the pines to cut them off, they rode down the lane. O'Toole took the lead, calling out to warn Sherrill and the others that he was coming.

Mickey was on duty at the stable and stepped out to wave them in. The wounded Ranger rode with head slumped. Relief in sight he could relax, and he felt his weariness, the aching pain in his side.

Esther Sherrill ran from the kitchen toward O'Toole, who was dismounting in the side yard. The two embraced, happiness overwhelming them. Dillard Sherrill, empty sleeve flapping, and several Loop S cowboys, came to greet the bedraggled pair from Rusk. Hatfield was down, loosening his cinches. He let the sweated saddle fall and gave his sorrel a loving slap. "Go on, run off and keep away from 'em, Goldy. I'll call when I want yuh." The handsome gelding trotted away with a snort. He would drink and graze, stay out of enemy clutches.

"Boss, Comanche Coombs and a passel of toughs are on top of us," warned O'Toole. "Inside, boys. Get set for a fight."

Penny and Dickie capered around, rollicking as usual. O'Toole herded everybody into the house and saw to it that men took their stations at windows and other loopholes. Sherrill gripped a Colt six-shooter in his hand.

Hatfield had practically hopped in, and he

sank into a kitchen chair. O'Toole spoke to Esther in a low tone and she nodded. Soon she brought hot coffee for the wounded officer. As he was drinking it, Hatfield heard the opening shots as Comanche Coombs bored in.

CHAPTER XII
PINNED DOWN

The warm drink revived Hatfield somewhat.
He could hear the gunfire had stepped up
and the Ranger noted that now it came from
all sides. "Hemmed us in," he thought.
Coombs had thrown a ring around the
Loop S buildings to pin them down. It was
as he had guessed. Doc Daniels was on the
prod and must destroy them or lose the
game.

"Could I have a basin of that hot water,
ma'am? And some clean cloths?"

· "Certainly."

Esther Sherrill had a big iron kettle steaming on the back of the cookstove. She
poured some into a tin basin and tore a
white cloth into strips. There was a small
room with a bunk in it off the kitchen. From
the sounds of the fight the Ranger could tell
that as yet there had been no concerted
rush.

His left leg was still numb and he had to

put most of his weight on his uninjured limb as he hopped to the bunk. Esther brought in the hot water and bandages, set them by him on a three-legged stool. He thanked her, looking up into the pretty, calm face.

"Yuh're a most beautiful lady," he told her softly. "And yuh got real spunk." There was no fear in Esther. She was a true pioneer woman.

She smiled down at him as he sat on the edge of the bunk. When she left, Hatfield went to work on himself. He gritted his teeth as he washed out bits of cloth and leather from the wound. It was a jagged, nasty looking furrow yet he was thankful that no bone had been splintered.

When he had cleansed the wound and re-bandaged it with the cloths Esther had given him, he lay down on his back to rest from the ordeal and shock. Gus O'Toole had promised to call him if there was need.

It was dark when the Ranger started awake. His left hip felt stiff as a board but though he was somewhat washed out, he was refreshed by his nap and new power was returning to his mighty being. Aware that trusted guards were on duty, the officer had been able to relax and sleep in the middle of clutching peril.

A faint streamer of yellow light filtered

under the bottom of the board door into the kitchen. He heard no shooting. Throughout the spacious ranch were quiet sounds, the murmur of talking men, the creak of a floor board, the occasional jangle of metal.

And to his widened nostrils came the smell of cooking food. He was really hungry and swung his legs around carefully so as not to break open the healing slash in his thigh.

Everybody at the Loop S was cheerful enough. Coombs had made no rush, only fired into the windows and doors. With the night, the guns had stopped talking but O'Toole had checked up, said they were still out there, holding in the defenders.

Guarded lights by which to reload weapons and move from point to point inside were set around the house. Esther was serving a late supper, fried potatoes and beef, biscuits and maple syrup, gravy, more coffee. Some stayed on watch while others ate, and Hatfield limped out in time to catch the second table. He was able to do more than justice to the hearty meal and the food gave him strength.

After dinner, the Ranger conferred with Sherrill and O'Toole. There was little to be done except arrange for sentries to rouse those who would sleep. O'Toole could attend to this, apportion the watches.

Down by the creek small fires showed that Coombs' men were cooking up a meal for themselves. Around ten Hatfield limped back to his bunk and turned in. Sleep was the best medicine and soon he drifted off.

Crackling shots, growing in volume, and a call from Gus O'Toole, at his door, brought the tall Ranger up. He pulled on his boots and strapped his cartridge belts around his narrow waist, put on his Stetson.

"They're comin'," reported O'Toole. "A bunch more rode up durin' the night."

It was now dawn, grayness over the rolling range. Hatfield found he could walk fairly well, though the jolts hurt him. He went with O'Toole to the living room where three Loop S waddies and Dillard Sherrill were crouching, carbines in hand, watching the enemy's approach.

The Ranger peeked from the edge of a window so as not to offer an easy target. "I see Coombs, and there's Doc Daniels and Razorback Kerr, stayin' well back." The gunslingers from Rusk had arrived, and there were new figures among them, no doubt taken on by Comanche and Daniels for the battle.

The big breed outlaw chief was among his men, urging them on, cursing at them but

Daniels and Kerr watched from a safe distance. The attackers picked up speed, digging their spurs deep and quirting their horses, down low over them. Dust billowed up and fierce howls came from brutal throats. Volleys from Colts and short-barreled rifles rattled and the defenders braced for the shock. They were coming from all directions, hoping to overrun the house.

But if they needed some light for such a rush, it also made it possible for those in the ranchhouse to pick targets. Scattered shots opened as Sherrill, Hatfield, O'Toole and the thinly set marksmen let go. A bandit caught a slug through the shoulder and screeched over the thundering din. The hoofs shook the earth.

Comanche Coombs, on a reddish-hided mustang, streaked in, swerved and rode down the south side to drive the outlaws there into the fray. Puffs of smoke came from windows and loopholes and a couple of horses dropped. Hatfield's cool, steady aim nicked at the weaving toughs. He jumped up and ran to another opening, taking a lead on Coombs. As he squeezed his carbine trigger, Comanche Coombs' cayuse shied from contact with another which spurted across its path. The Ranger's bullet hit the horse instead of the man.

Coombs was a magnificent rider. He felt the terrible bound as the animal under him caught the lead. Kicking his booted feet loose from the stirrups, Comanche jumped for it and landed running. He zigzagged and the horses of the charging outlaws protected him from the Ranger's followers.

Coombs made the stable and dove around its protecting corner. He had not been wounded but the fact he was no longer out there, egging his followers to it, dampened the spirits of the killers. The stinging lead from the house, their inability to see whether they were doing any damage to the defenders, turned the tide. Instead of coming all the way in, those in the van jerked rein and pelted past, shooting into the windows with wild bursts.

"That shore fizzled out!" chuckled Dillard Sherrill, blowing smoke from his carbine barrel as he reloaded. "Without Comanche they're nothin'."

"That kind just don't like frontal attacks," drawled the Ranger.

Those behind were only looking for an excuse to turn and before long they had all withdrawn outside easy range. Doc Daniels was talking at them, hands gesticulating, showing his digusted rage.

"Wonder what's next?" said Sherrill.

"They'll chew it over for a while," guessed Hatfield.

He was right. The eastern sky was flaming red as the new sun started up. Comanche Coombs, who had borrowed another mount, rode over and held a confab with Doc Daniels. The breed kept shrugging, looking now and then toward the ranch-house.

Down by the creek, knots of the outlaws collected and built cookfires of dry wood. Breakfast was in order and they spiked their coffee from bottles they had brought along. Wolfish eyes watched the Loop S. After a while, receiving special orders from Daniels and Coombs, a dozen men mounted and rode off toward Rusk.

"They got an idea. Wonder what it could be?" mused the Ranger.

"Makes me hungry to watch those cusses," announced Sherrill. "Esther! How about grub?"

"I've got breakfast started, father," the young woman called from the kitchen.

They were held in the house as the patrols of Coombs' followers moved here and there. In the middle of the morning there was some sort of alarm, a rider coming down the creek, yelling and waving his Stetson. A score of armed gunhands hustled back with Comanche leading them. Before long the defenders caught the crackle of gunfire beyond the north slopes.

"Huh!" grunted the Ranger. "I wonder if that's the JayBee tryin' to make it here?"

If Jake Butler and Art Gerdes, Sherrill's neighbors, failed to come with sufficient force they would be beaten off on the open range.

The day dragged along. It was very hot, a haze over the land. "It's goin' to rain," declared Sherrill. "I can feel it. My arm stub always aches."

Watchers took turns at the peepholes but the enemy did not again come at the house. It was not until late that afternoon that the Ranger found out what Doc Daniels' idea was. The gunhands who had been sent off toward Rusk early that morning returned, driving a dozen long wagons. These were parked near the creek bank and men with axes began cutting six-inch thick pines, trimming off the branches. A barricade heavy enough to stop bullets was constructed around each wagon.

"I see," nodded Hatfield. "They're comin' in behind 'em." Each wagon would hold a dozen men or more, lying back of the crude shields. Rawhide lengths lashed the horizon-

153

tal logs to uprights at each corner of a vehicle.

His keen eye did not miss the buckets and small casks which had been fetched in the carts. "Coal oil, I s'pose, and pitch," he told Dillard Sherrill. "Yore walls are wooden and they'll burn fine with kerosene on 'em!"

The plan of the coming attack was now plain to them and anxiety smote their hearts. Smoked out they would fall easy prey to the vicious guns.

Save for the volleys heard earlier there was no sign of help coming from the other ranches.

Dark descended, but no stars, no moon showed in the heavens. They were murky, the air heavy as all breeze had died away. "What's that?" asked Gus O'Toole.

"Sounds like thunder," said Mickey.

"Mebbe it's them heavy wagons comin'," suggested Sherrill.

Uneasy hands clutched weapons, Colts and carbines, ready for the clash.

"It's thunder! And here comes the carts, too!" announced Jim Hatfield.

They had been finishing supper but they all quit and ran to their stations. From the intense darkness came the grumble of big wheels. Doc Daniels was starting for them again. Hatfield tried with his carbine, firing by ear. If his bullets hit anything it was not human. The wagons came slowly on. It was eerie waiting there, wondering what came next.

"Here's the wind!" said Dillard Sherrill.

Gusts struck the low-lying building, and the dust whirled into the air. Inside of minutes the breeze had reached gale force, driving from the southeast, a storm bellowing in off the mighty Gulf. There was a violent flash of lightning, and for a breath those inside could see the carts, the drivers handling the reins as they crouched behind the log sides. Hatfield threw metal at one of the teams, heard a screaming response, but then the lightning went out.

The thunder reverberated in the tense air, shaking the earth.

Over the sounds of the approaching storm came shouted orders, and the gunslingers howled in triumph. Cans and buckets of kerosene were hurled against the wooden walls, and the defenders' fire had little effect, the lead stopped by the pine logs around the wagons.

Matches lighted pitch-soaked torches dipped into the oil and these were lobbed against the house, some starting blazes which licked up at the dry wood.

Chapter XIII
Storm

The storm burst full upon them. The lightning all around the house and the mighty thundering deafened them, drowning out the crackle of the guns.

At the same time hope sprang into the hearts of those in the ranchhouse. They heard the big drops of rain and as the gale shrieked to full force the clouds opened and it poured. On the roof sounded a tattoo as large hailstones mingled with the rain.

Hatfield moved over to Dillard Sherrill, crouching by the front door. When the lightning flashed, everybody in the place would shoot. "Sherrill!" said the Ranger. "I'm goin' out, it's my chance in this storm."

"What for? The rain will douse those fires, Hatfield."

"Yeah, it will save us this time. But this wagon trick will work soon as it dries out tomorrow! We must find more fightin' men."

It was a deluge, the heavy rain driven in

sheets against the walls, soaking them, wetting the ground and checking the incipient blazes the killers had started. Most of the long wagons turned, drawing off. A dead horse had to be cut from the harness of two before the vehicles could shift.

Defeated by the storm, Comanche Coombs and Daniels drew off. The yard rapidly became a shallow lake, the packed earth failing to sop up the water. Hatfield had been slowed by the wound he had taken in Rusk, but now he had regained his mastery and power. He tightened his gunbelts at his waist, and left his Stetson behind, binding his black locks with a bandanna. Blacking from Esther's can of stove polish in the kitchen stained his face and cut the sheen of flesh.

Ready, he crawled from a window, crouching there for an instant. Then he jumped up, splashing through the pools of rain. He reached a corral and vaulted the fence. As he did so chain lightning ran along the ground like a live thing, the thunder roaring its fury, and hailstones as big as pigeon eggs pelted him.

Some of the outlaws sighted the running figure in the flashes. They were coming for him but he seized the mane of a shivering mustang, frightened by the tempest, and pulled himself to the beast's bare back. Gripping with his knees, he rode to a gate, kicked open the catch bar, and went through.

It was a wild run, and pistols stabbed at him. The howls and explosions were vague in the shrieking wind and the noise of rampaging nature.

That afternoon Hatfield had glimpsed Goldy on the hills across the creek, but it was manifestly impossible to whistle up his golden sorrel in the crashing din. He swerved and headed easterly from the ranchhouse, soon lost in the inky, moving air and drenched from head to foot. He had trouble guiding the dark Loop S mustang, who was terrified of the thunder and lightning. He used his knees, gripped the shaggy mane with one hand. He had brought a hackamore in his pocket and when he felt he could afford to slow, he managed to work it into place by sense of touch, the warm, heaving wet cayuse under him. . . .

In an hour the storm had passed. The wind was abating, coming in cool gusts and the air had cleared. He looked up and saw stars between the racing black clouds. Not long after this he was able to identify the Big Dipper and so set his course. Soon he cut the red highway, the depressions filled with water, which ran between Rusk and Nacogdoches. The hackamore serving as a bridle, he pushed on for the latter settlement.

When the dawn came up, Hatfield was close to the old town. He sighted curls of smoke as breakfast fires were being lighted in the homes. On the heights over Nacogdoches, Hatfield could see along a stretch of road, and the approach of a large band of riders stopped him as he studied the figures coming his way.

With a satisfied grunt, the Ranger kicked his heels against the dark mustang's ribs and hurried on.

In the lead were Buck Robertson, on Old Heart 7, and the blunt man from Waco, Angus Dunn. It was to Dunn that the Ranger had sent his wire, carried to the Nacogdoches telegraph by Buck Robertson. While awaiting Dunn, Buck had had time to eat, sleep and rest the chunky gray.

Dunn wore a white shirt and corduroy pants thrust into shiny halfboots. The brim of his black hat was narrow, and he carried a new carbine and had a Colt strapped at his waist. His face was always florid but his manner had undergone a radical change. "Ranger!" He thrust out his hand, grinning in pleasure. "I didn't know who you were, you understand that. I had your message and brought every man I could pick up." He waved back at his armed forces.

Buck had further set Angus Dunn on the right track as to the tall man, after they had met at Nacogdoches. Dunn had come on the first train he could catch and had hired mounts after arriving at his destination.

All of Dunn's coal operators were on hand, those who had been bullied by Doc Daniels in Waco, including the oldster who looked pleased at being included in the party. And Dunn had trusted employes, armed to the teeth and at his command.

"You think we can really down 'em, Ranger?" asked Dunn eagerly, as Hatfield turned his horse and they started northwest for the Loop S.

"We shore will try, suh."

Angus Dunn studied the rugged, grim face of the tall officer. Hatfield was hatless, his cheeks smudged by blacking. It was all out, Dunn understood. They must defeat Doc Daniels or Dunn and all his associates would pay the price. Daniels would not offer them another chance.

The sun came up behind them, turning a hot golden color, drying out the land after the storm. Broken branches, strewn leaves and washouts showed the force of the rain

160

and hail. Hatfield, aware of the critical situation at the Loop S, kept pushing up the pace as they cantered along. Daniels' trick with the wagons would succeed, with the house wall ready to take fire.

"Yuh reckon we're a mile from Sherrill's now, Buck?" inquired the Ranger. The miles had clicked off under the beating hoofs of the determined avengers.

"I'd say so, Jim. I remember that big red cliff over there, it wasn't long after I left yuh that I seen it."

"We'll take to the range, then."

They followed the tall officer, all eager to do his bidding. The silver star on silver circle gleamed on his shirt, emblem of his great organization.

"I'd shore like to have a few more men, especially cowboy riders," he thought. Dunn and his type could fight bravely and well afoot but while they could handle a horse, as could every Texan, they did not have the skill needed in a running brawl, shooting from a jolting saddle, whooping it up.

His keen ear heard the spattering gunfire, it came from a northerly direction. He could see curls of black smoke drifting up from the position of the ranchhouse, and feared that the brutal, crushing attack was even now beginning.

As they came up over a rise and past a clump of piney woods they sighted some of Comanche Coombs' outlaws, shooting at a score of horsemen who had pulled up to reply.

"There's Jake Butler, owner of the JayBee Ranch," said Hatfield. "We can use those waddies!"

They spurted over, shooting as they struck the bandits on the flank. Dunn and the rest trailed the Ranger and their metal and battle cries soon started the foe running back to Sherrill's.

Jake Butler raised an arm, signaling the Ranger and Buck, whom he had met in Rusk. The two parties joined and rapidly exchanged information. "This is the third stab we made tryin' to reach the Loop S," the heavy-set Butler told Hatfield. "We were driven off. Say, Ranger, meet Art Gerdes of the Shark brand." Gerdes was small in stature but alert, smooth shaven, a plug of tobacco bulging one leathery cheek. He had quick blue eyes which smiled at the tall officer from Austin.

"We're with yuh, Ranger," declared Gerdes. "Our spreads ain't too big, but we brought all the men we could. Had to leave a few on guard since from what yuh told Butler we're likely to be hit any minute."

Hatfield nodded. "I'm glad yuh're here, suh, and the same goes for yuh, Mister Butler. We have a tough job, and I only hope we make the Loop S on time. Come along and I'll put yuh up to date as we ride."

He was anxious about Sherrill's fate. It was dried out now after the storm and there was more and more smoke rising over the ranch. Led by the mighty Ranger the reinforced party hurried along.

Not far ahead quirted the band of gunhands which had been assigned to fend off Sherrills's neighbors.

Hatfield told Butler and Gerdes what had occurred. The two listened intently, grunting angrily now and then as the full story of Doc Daniels' perfidy emerged. They realized that they were to be next, with Sherrill disposed of.

They skirted a pine woods and started up a long slope, with the fleeing outlaws at the top. A golden gelding broke from the evergreens, whinnying as he picked up speed and overtook the Ranger. "Goldy! Come here, boy," called Hatfield. It was his war horse, watching for him.

He transferred to the big sorrel. They could hear confused shouts and heavy gunfire beyond. At the crest they sighted the ranchhouse. Daniels was again essaying his wagon trick. Against the walls were the barricaded carts, filled with prostrate fighters pouring lead through the billowing oil smoke.

Hatfield quickly estimated the situation. Down by the creek were bunches of enemy horses, holders gripping reins. The outlaws just ahead were yelling and signaling to their friends, warning of the Ranger's approach, but so intent were Coombs and his bullies on the job that the avengers were within two hundred yards before the bulk of attackers saw them.

"Get down there and stampede those mustangs, Mister Butler," ordered Hatfield. "Take a dozen of yore men. Rest of yuh string out and foller me."

Bareback on the magnificent sorrel, guns loaded, Jim Hatfield prepared for the crashing battle.

Chapter XIV
Guns at the Loop S

Comanche Coombs still held the advantage of numbers in spite of the reinforcements picked up on the way in. But the men behind the Ranger were of different type from Coombs' hirelings. They were furious, mad clean through at what had been done to them by the outlaws. They were fighting for their homes, for life itself, for their loved ones.

Well spaced according to Hatfield's directions, the rescuers picked up speed and howled their warcries. From the backs of their horses they could shoot into the wagons and their lead began slashing at the killers lying behind the log sides. The black, oily smoke, burning kerosene and pitch hurled against the house walls, wafted up into the golden air.

Art Butler and a dozen hard riders were sweeping to the creek, yelling and shooting. The outlaws' mustangs were beginning to dance, the holders having trouble as the powerful beasts jerked at the tangled reins.

Hatfield was out ahead. Buck was off to his left, the light youth riding Old Heart 7 with reckless abandon, his face alive with the excitement of the scrap. Angus Dunn and Art Gerdes, the coal operators and their friends, the cowboys, were driving forward.

The mounted bandits they had chased in stayed in their saddles, swerving and pelting past the stable and house, shouting the alarm. Now Coombs and his gun-hands hastily turned as they felt the burning metal from the Ranger's direction. Slugs shrieked past the incoming attackers.

Hatfield's cool, gray-green eyes watched the development of the conflict, sizing it up. He had a field general's ability in such actions. He was glad to see puffs of gunsmoke from several windows, for it told him that Sherrill, O'Toole and the handful inside the house were still able to resist.

"Hit 'em just right," he muttered, taking aim at a seething wagonload of killers.

Comanche Coombs was over there, Hatfield recognized the tall figure. He swerved Goldy so that he might clash personally with Coombs. The sunlight glinted from the Ranger badge and Hatfield gave a shrill Rebel yell to attract Comanche's attention.

Heavy volleys smashed the warm air. As the outlaws saw the Ranger's forces coming they deserted the wagons for the low sides did not fully shield them. "Look like rats leavin' a sinkin' ship," thought Hatfield, grim as he closed.

They were hunting cover but they were panicked because their horses were not at hand. A means of escape was the first requisite of such fellows. Most of them ran through the smoke, turning to fire as they scurried off. Hatfield was in the thickest of the smoke and could no longer see past the ranchhouse to the line of trees along the stream.

He kept his eye on Comanche Coombs who was holding a hot Colt in one big hand and cursing his running friends.

Hatfield did not see Doc Daniels. The uneven line of horsemen, wings pinching in, swept up, violent blasts of their weapons completing the rout.

Comanche Coombs darted around the stable. Most of his men had rushed past him, on the way to their mustangs. Hatfield saw the breed disappear behind the building, and he veered the golden gelding.

As he tore past the corner, Coombs loomed before him, mounted on a long-legged, steel-hued horse.

Hatfield's rush carried him within a few jumps of Coombs who was swinging his horse to retreat along the lane.

"Pull up and throw down, Coombs!" bellowed the officer.

Comanche had to jerk hard on his rein, pull his mustang around to face his enemy. "Hanford! Ranger, I'll kill yuh!" he shrieked.

He was very fast and he held a cocked Colt in one hand. Hatfield had given the warning which all Rangers offered even to the worst of outlaws. Coombs refused to heed it. All the maddened man could think of was his hate. His high-boned cheeks worked, his mouth was set, the black Indian eyes were crimson.

It was man to man at this instant, the elemental savagery of Comanche Coombs completely possessing the killer's being. The Rangers wanted this terrible bandit, who had proved a scourge wherever he lighted. So far Coombs had emerged triumphant over what forces the law had sent against him.

The officer's pistol and the fancy Colt of Comanche Coombs seemed to speak together. Hatfield saw a surprised look cross Coombs' dark face. The black eyes flickered. He heard the whine of a heavy slug past his ear as he sent a second one into the breed as a precaution. This rocked Comanche whose arm was dropping.

The steel-colored gelding snorted and reared straight up, stampeded by the explosions so close to his ears. Coombs slid from his saddle and heaped on the worn dirt beyond the stable doors.

The Ranger, after checking the field chief of the outlaws, hurried on down to the creek. Jake Butler had done a fine job of it. The few holders had been gunned off and forced to release the mustangs which had split up and run in every direction, abetted by the whoops and shooting of the JayBee and Shark. Buck and a number of Dunn's fighters had swept past the smoking ranch-house.

Terrified gunhands, bereft of mounts and caught in the open by the yelling, menacing band, threw down their weapons and themselves, hoping to escape death by adject surrender.

"Take their guns and hold 'em, Mister Dunn," shouted Hatfield.

He waved to his friends, seeing that all was well on the level area along the creek. Turning Goldy, he trotted back to the ranchhouse. Gerdes and others had dismounted and made some prisoners of wounded or stunned outlaws, while Dillard

Sherrill, Gus O'Toole and other defenders were hurrying out to greet the rescuers.

"Yuh made it, Ranger," cried O'Toole, throwing his Stetson high in the air. "I told 'em yuh'd come in time."

Eyes were smarting, they were coughing from the smoke. The wooden walls were afire. "Better organize bucket lines and pronto. Put some of them cusses to work, O'Toole," ordered Hatfield.

"A good idea!" O'Toole rushed off to fight the blaze and save Sherrill's home.

They were carrying out Mrs. Sherrill on a cot. Penny and Dickie scampered around the yard, yelling in the excitement. The guns were dying away as the bandits quit in droves, those fortunate enough to have been in their saddles riding for the tall timber.

Esther was with her mother, seeing to her. Hatfield got down, dropped rein. His saddle was hanging on a rack near the barn, undamaged as he had left it. He cleaned up, put on his Stetson, and slapped the hull on Goldy. Everybody was helping now to throw water on the burning log walls of the house. A long string of bucket passing men stretched to the creek, among them numbers of the captive outlaws, forced to assist by the armed victors.

Gus O'Toole was bossing the job. He was

near the house, steam issuing from the hot wood as water was hurled in.

"Have yuh seen Doc Daniels?" inquired Hatfield.

O'Toole turned, his smoke-stained face runneled by sweat. "He was here half an hour ago, I saw him down by the creek just before yuh come along, Ranger. Razorback Kerr was with him."

"I'm goin' after him, Gus. Soon as yuh get the fire under control yuh better head for Rusk with Dunn and a dozen or so of the boys. See yuh."

He was impelled by an uneasy urgency to overtake Doc Daniels. Instinct warned him that his most dangerous foe was eluding him and he was forced to start on Daniels' trail. He rode along the lane and swung west for the settlement in which Doc Daniels had spun his web.

CHAPTER XV
REPORT

The sun was low in the sky beyond Rusk, the tall pines black silhouettes against the light, as the Ranger rode down into town. His eyes cast from side to side, expecting trouble. Some of Coombs' gunhands had escaped at the Loop S and Daniels had forces of his own.

Keeping to the center of the wide main artery, Jim Hatfield rode north, watching for his foes. He passed the Dutchman's and there were men inside, drinking, but none disputed his progress. He stared at the Rusk House, hoping to see Anita Robertson, but she was not in view. He was in a hurry, wishing to come up with Daniels. Duty was the first impelling urge of the tall officer.

"Mebbe he had loot to pick up at his house," he mused, chinstrap taut under his rugged jaw, the lines of his face drawn. That wound dealt him had sapped his physical strength but he was traveling on his indomitable will.

He reached the mansion at the north end of the town. In the distance he heard the whistle of an approaching train, heading south for Rusk junction.

Daniels' home was deserted, even the servants had fled. He lost several minutes checking there before he remounted and trotted the sorrel back to the center. The train's warning sounded, closer to Rusk.

He dropped rein in front of the Rusk House. "Mebbe Anita will have spotted the cuss," he thought.

"Miss Robertson, suh?" repeated the desk clerk. "She just went out with Mister Kerr. Do yuh know him?"

"I know him." The clerk had seen Hatfield before, for Buck and the officer had stayed there. But now the tall man wore the Ranger star and the story of the big fight was going through town.

Hatfield was inwardly alarmed although no sign showed in his manner. Razorback Kerr was Daniels' chief aide. "How about Doc Daniels? Yuh seen him too?" he drawled.

"He done rode past just before Mister Kerr went upstairs after the lady. Had a carpetbag before him, Ranger."

Hatfield knew they had seen Anita with

him in town; and Daniels would not be above using her as a hostage if he could save himself that way. Kerr might have tricked her into going with him or else held a hidden gun in his pocket as he forced her outside.

As he hit the wooden sidewalk and ducked under the long hitchrail the train pulled in at the station, brakes squeaking, engine stack puffing cindery smoke. Loafers down the line had stepped over to watch the people get off the cars or board the southbound express.

"Carpetbag! He's on his way," decided the Ranger, foot in the stirrup.

The train would not remain long at Rusk. People were about on the walks, in the bars and stores, saddle horses and vehicles were in the roads. Men stared at the tall Ranger moving south along Main Avenue to the depot.

Suddenly he sighted Razorback Kerr. The metal master sat a gray horse and close by him, on a white gelding, was Anita Robertson, her golden hair trim on her head. They were watching as he came down the road. A bulging side wall had hidden them until Hatfield reached this point.

"Ranger!" Kerr's rusty voice was thin. In one hand he held a cocked revolver which

174

he had pulled from his pocket.

"Watch out, Jim!" screamed Anita. "Keep away."

She was hoping to save her friend. For Hatfield could not shoot Kerr without endangering the woman's life, Razorback kept partially behind her and at that range a pistol slug might swerve enough to strike her.

The train whistled, warning it was on its way. Hatfield pulled the golden sorrel around and headed straight toward Kerr. He held his rein in his left hand and his right rested on his leather-sheathed hip, close to the heavy revolver.

Razorback Kerr's hunched back gave him a dwarfish aspect when he was in the saddle. His piggish eyes were riveted to the Ranger, who slowly kept coming. "Stay away or I'll fire," shrieked Kerr.

Hatfield's icy gray-green eyes held Kerr. He did not speak as he moved in.

It took sheer steel nerve and mustard to ride at a pointed gun without showing the slightest flicker of anxiety but Hatfield did it. He believed that Razorback Kerr would crack.

He had read the man perfectly. The pistol muzzle wavered and Kerr's arm slowly dropped. He bit his lip, no longer able to meet that gray-green stare.

"All right, cuss it! I ain't goin' to stretch rope for Daniels. He made me stick here so he could run clear."

Razorback Kerr's loyalty had undergone a terrific wrench as he had found himself relegated to the role of burnt sacrifice to save Doc Daniels.

Hatfield came around, reached out and pulled the Colt out the of limp fingers. "Here, Anita. Keep him on deck till I come back. Shoot if he tries to run."

"Yes, Jim. I knew you'd come." The girl had strength and a pioneer woman's determination. She could handle firearms and accepted the responsibility of holding Razorback Kerr prisoner for her Ranger friend.

"All a-board!" The conductor's attenuated warning sounded from the depot.

Doc Daniels was on that southbound express, bound for new fields to conquer. Hatfield galloped Goldy the remaining distance, rounding the station toward the puffing engine. The hand brakes had been released and the slow *choo-choo* smote the warm air, couplings jerking as the train started off.

The station loafers gawked as the powerful golden gelding streaked into sight, hoofs pounding across the wooden platform and taking to the cinder ballast along the right-of-way. They watched the magnificent rider with the Ranger star as he seized a handrail at the rear of the last car and with wiry ease swung aboard.

Doc Daniels came at him, shooting the length of the passenger car. He had been peering from an open window up the train and glimpsed the Ranger as the latter made it. Men, women and children in the seats at either side of the aisle crouched low, crying out in alarm as the heavy reports roared in the coach.

Daniels was in a fury. His wide, heavy body was clad in a black suit, white shirt and collar, string tie. His hat was off, exposing the balcony brow, the thin brown hair greased to the unpleasant skull. His eyes bulged with the glare of a maddened sea monster, phosphorescent with rage.

There could never be any surrender on Daniels' part. He knew that the Ranger would relentlessly hound him to the hangman's noose, never relax until Daniels was through. The evil which the chief had done could never be excused.

Limping, thrown off balance by the jolting train as it picked up speed, Jim Hatfield felt the close whine of the bullets pouring from Daniels' leveled six-shooter. Six-gun

Junction was certainly living up to its name.

Other passengers had hurriedly ducked as the noisy duel flared in the car. A woman shrilly screamed, and a man roared, "Cut that out! Cut that out!" There were small ones too, and a baby began to cry.

With the Ranger on the train Doc Daniels' only chance was to down the officer, and he knew it. Hatfield paused, offering a fair target but gripping the nearby seat back with his left hand so he could steady himself against the uneasy motion. The Ranger pistol came up, hammer spur back under the long thumb.

He had the impression of Daniels' cruel, twisted features, and Doc's gun kept exploding, a slug whipping a chunk of felt from his Stetson brim. Then Hatfield raised his thumb and the six-shooter pushed against his palm.

Doc Daniels pitched on, stumbling, whirling, flung on by his own momentum and the gathering speed. For the last few feet he seemed to be flying through the air. He crashed hard, sliding up to Hatfield's spread feet and then the Ranger himself was thrown down, saving himself by his clutch on the seat.

Somebody had pulled the stop cord and the engineer had jammed on his brakes.

Everybody was jerked so his neck nearly snapped and many brought up against the seat ahead.

Hatfield came up on one knee, pulled himself erect. He checked Doc Daniels, picked up the revolver which had fallen from his foe's hand. A conductor came running through from the next coach.

"What's goin' on in here?" he shouted excitedly.

Then he stared at the tall man wearing the silver star on silver circle. "Oh howdy, Ranger. Yuh got on at Six-gun Junction, I reckon. . . ." In Captain William McDowell's Austin headquarters, Jim Hatfield sat smoking a quirly as he reported to his superior officer.

McDowell listened with the keenest relish, enjoying vicarious thrills as he imagined the events so tersely described by Hatfield. McDowell had worked on outlaws and Indian problems when he was younger and he could picture just what had gone on.

"So Comanche Coombs is pushin' up daisies in Boot Hill, huh? And yuh finished off this Porter Daniels, he was a wild man, no foolin'. The janitor in Hades will be mighty busy."

"Yes suh. Razorback Kerr, Daniels' expert, turned state's evidence. He says Daniels and

Coombs killed Fant Wright, and others over there as they seized control, Cap'n. We busted up Coombs' crew, caught a bunch and the rest scattered for it. Six-gun Junction should calm down now. Sherrill and the other ranchers are safe. This Gus O'Toole, who runs the Loop S for Sherrill, gave us a real hand. He'll see to it that rich iron ore under the Loop S and the neighborin' range is put to good use."

"Iron! I'd say it's the most important metal there is, Hatfield," declared McDowell. "They're usin' it more and more, with the railroads pokin' through the land and the barbed wire bein' strung."

"Daniels had big orders for wire, Cap'n, and for rails, for ship plates, and other vital products. Had to fill 'em. Yuh savvy there was a foundry at Rusk durin' the War but it petered out on account there wasn't enough fuel for the forges. The comin' of the railroads made it possible to bring in coal and Daniels figgered it all out. He put the screws on Angus Dunn and his pards to make 'em furnish fuel cheap. He was grabbin' the iron deposits from the ranchers, and snatched Fant Wright's old foundry, with Razorback Kerr in charge of production. Comanche Coombs and his bunch handled the strongarm work."

Buck and Anita Robertson were safe at their Austin cottage after the dangerous days in Rusk. Hatfield had brought the law to Six-gun Junction and the surrounding range. The iron ore would more than pay for the property damage done at the Loop S.

The sun shone brightly over the capital, heart of the Lone Star empire. McDowell always had work for a Ranger and Hatfield was never so content as when he was on the trail, riding against the foes of the State.

In the days since he had tamed Rusk, Hatfield's wound had healed and he could walk with scarcely any limp. He had rested and was ready to ride.

Soon the mighty Ranger took leave of his captain, swinging into the golden gelding's saddle. They were away again, carrying the law to teeming, vast Texas.

We hope you have enjoyed this Large Print book. Other Thorndike, Wheeler, and Chivers Press Large Print books are available at your library or directly from the publishers.

For information about current and upcoming titles, please call or write, without obligation, to:

Publisher
Thorndike Press
295 Kennedy Memorial Drive
Waterville, ME 04901
Tel. (800) 223-1244

or visit our Web site at:

www.gale.com/thorndike
www.gale.com/wheeler

OR

Chivers Large Print
published by BBC Audiobooks Ltd
St James House, The Square
Lower Bristol Road
Bath BA2 3SB
England
Tel. +44(0) 800 136919
email: bbcaudiobooks@bbc.co.uk
www.bbcaudiobooks.co.uk

All our Large Print titles are designed for easy reading, and all our books are made to last.